The Moon Butter Route

Max Yoho

The Moon Butter Route

Max Yoho

Dancing Goat Press
Topeka, Kansas

The Moon Butter Route

For Information address: Dancing Goat Press
3013 SW Quail Creek Dr., Topeka, Kansas 66614

www.dancinggoatpress.com

PRINTING HISTORY
First Printing, Nov. 2005
ISBN 0-9708160-4-9

PRINTED IN THE UNITED STATES OF AMERICA
BY HALL COMMERCIAL PRINTING, TOPEKA, KANSAS

For Carol,
whose constant support and hard work made it happen.

And with special thanks to
Naomi Patterson, Carol Ann Robb, Bill Shaffer,
and to my editor
Karen Sells Brown.

Author's Note

November 2, 1880: Kansas voters ratified an amendment to the state constitution prohibiting the "manufacture and sale of intoxicating liquors…except for medical, scientific and mechanical purposes."

July 8, 1949: The first truckload of legal liquor arrives in Kansas following repeal of prohibition against sale of alcohol.

1

The trouble began when that old black Packard hearse rolled up to the only stop sign in town. It stopped briefly, but briefly was long enough for the danged goat I was chasing to jump to the hood, then to the top of that Packard and start peeing on it. I'm glad my mom wasn't there. I would have been crucified, dead, and buried for letting one of our goats pee on a Packard. But, see, goats are absolutely indiscriminate.

Just below the tin roof, in a fine varnished coffin, rested the dignified, if now pretty much useless remains of Reverend Walter Walters. Likely, when he was alive, he could have preached a two-hour sermon concerning the indignity of such a desecration.

Sam Pullium was not a member of Reverend Walters' flock, and some folks didn't speak well of him. But in all fairness, Sam had a thoughtful view of the way things ought to be done. Doubtless in Sam's mind, a funeral procession that included a goat peeing on the top of a Packard hearse was *not* the way things ought to be done. Anyway, what with the Japs and the Nazis, the police and other undesirables, Sam had had enough. Therefore, he pulled a nickel-plated .32 caliber Iver Johnson revolver from beneath his vest and shot my dad's goat completely dead. With one bullet he eradicated one-third of my problems in life. About three more bullets flew, making it plain to everyone that Sam intended to uphold the high standards of Epic, Kansas. If it bothered anyone that Sam was making up his own standards of what was right or wrong for Epic—*per gratis, per diem, per* better stand back—nobody stepped forward to complain.

If I could have just borrowed Sam's revolver and shot two more bullets and killed two more goats, my summer would have looked like the gold-pot end of a rainbow.

I knew I might catch Hail Columbia from my dad. It was my summer job to keep three danged goats under control, but it is my firm belief that no human person can control a goat. This one had slipped his leather neck collar and bounded away toward town quicker than quick. But I was weeding and patching up the mulch in the strawberry patch right beside him. When he ran, I was on his tail like a piece of lightning.

Nevertheless, that old goat got himself on the top of the hearse and got himself killed dead, and it was not my fault.

His blood dripped even more desecration than the aforementioned desecration above the final remains of a man so kind and gentle that he would not hurt his own mother.

Now, here in Epic, there are people skilled in all manner of pursuits, but those with experience in pulling a shot goat off a Packard hearse while Sam Pullium was taking pot shots with a nickel-plated revolver appeared to be in limited supply that day. And it's not like the danged goat had the decorum to just be shot and tumble off that hearse. Oh, no, he dropped like a rock and lay on the top of that Packard as if he had been designed there on a drawing board at the Packard Motor Company. Goats are a cross to bear. Whoever it was that first depicted the Devil as resembling a goat just plain knew his goats.

Nevertheless, I believe Reverend Walters would have been pleased to get the extra attention.

Inside the hearse the undertaker, old man C. W. Brown, carefully eased out the clutch and tested the traffic. The Packard moved out grudgingly, as if the trip to the cemetery had ceased to be an adventure. It likely had. There are more folks lying in the cemetery than there are walking the streets in Epic.

Mr. Brown was deaf as the underside of a Frigidaire and nearly as blind. He had not heard the shots from Sam Pullium's revolver. Neither had he heard the goat dying on the roof of the Packard. So he pointed the hearse in the general direction of the cemetery, trying each side of the road without prejudice. Maybe he was determined to find the smoothest route for the Reverend; maybe he was just determined to find the road.

If only to see what in the world would happen next, I trotted along behind.

When my dad brought those danged goats home, he explained my responsibilities: I was to feed them and water them and catch them when they escaped. And they did escape! If tied by a rope, they would chew through it. If chained, I'll swear, they would find a hammer and cold-chisel and cut through it. Goats are a terrible burden to lay on a boy. The lesson to be learned from goats is this: even God makes mistakes.

In my opinion, parental advisability often falls short of the mark. My dad never mentioned what I should do in case one of our goats happened to escape and get shot dead while peeing on the roof of a black Packard hearse containing the mortal remains of Reverend Walter Walters. Because it was never discussed, I had no contingency plan. It was not my fault. The best I could do was trot along behind that long Packard, hoping for the best but not expecting it.

Still, I wasn't too worried. My dad was not a great supporter of Reverend Walters. Reverend Walters had once happened along when my dad was adjusting the bands on the planetary transmission of our Model T Ford. When my dad did that job, he used words, as well as tools, to help him through the ordeal. He was using some of those words when the Reverend stepped up behind him. I just guess that old preacher had never adjusted the bands on a Model T or he would have been more understanding. I was there. I saw my dad bang his head on the steering wheel when the Reverend spoke right in his ear, offering words of rebuke and only the barest hope of salvation.

I have no idea what the voice of the Holy Ghost sounds like, but if it sounds as raspy and unpleasant as Reverend Walters, then I expect words such as "Blasphemy!" being shouted would cause a good many heads to be bumped on steering wheels.

I watched as my dad pulled his skinned and bloody knuckles from the guts of that transmission. I was there, and on that day I learned words which would later prove to be of value in dealing with the handling of three danged goats. Goats and Model T transmissions have much in common.

Likely Reverend Walters had already heard most of Dad's words; but if he had ever heard them strung together in such a mellifluous and professional way, I would be very much surprised. I watched him walk away in deep and ponderous thought. No doubt Reverend Walters was figuring a way to include a segment on adjusting the bands of a Model T planetary transmission in his next sermon.

It was hot as sin at the cemetery, and I figured that old roof-goat would soon commence to ripen. I really wished my dad were with me. He would likely have whispered into my ear about the sanctified pleasure of a goat being sacrificed to ease the Reverend on his glorious way to whatever was to be his next experience.

Sam Pullium did not come with the procession. Doubtless he believed he had done enough to improve the world for one day. If anyone thought Sam had done less than enough, they darn sure did not step forward and complain.

The black Packard hearse stopped a few feet from the grave hole, and old man C. W. Brown crawled out. He wore a long, solemn, undertaker face. I would bet he had rehearsed that face for years in front of a cheval glass. His face bespoke that he would rather chop off a toe than endure the pain of burying Reverend Walters. But I'm sure he expected to end the day with his feet propped up thanking God for the miracle of death.

Yes, Mr. Brown was deaf. He was also so near blind that he should not have been driving a black Packard hearse. But no one would tell him that. Plain old common good sense tells you not to offend your undertaker. If you do, just as he closes the coffin lid, he will twist your nose slanch-wise or pull your mouth into a leer, and then Saint Peter will just tell you to go to Hell.

It was then Mr. Brown noticed the goatly remains on his roof, dripping blood and desecration in all directions. It was running down that little gutter-type thing along the side. But also, it spread only inches above the defenseless body of Reverend Walter Walters.

I just guess that if C.W. Brown had been able to come up with a nickel-plated revolver of his own, he would have killed that poor old goat all over again.

Ed Sutherland, the fellow who digs the grave holes in the cemetery, is not one to be intimidated by a goat, be it live or be it dead. He grabbed my dad's former goat by a hind leg and pulled its inappropriateness from the top of the hearse, without a blink or a hiccup.

Ed is a good man and takes pride in the holes he digs. He digs them straight, he digs them deep, and it would be a pretty sour person to not be pleased to be buried in one of them. The folks he was fond of and the folks he was not fond of all got fine holes to rest in. That's the kind of man he is.

However, his lack of experience in dead goat removal manifested itself as the hooves and horns of the goat scraped across the enamel of the black Packard. C.W. Brown was near blind, but not so blind that he couldn't see those gouges.

"You are a stupid S.O.B.!" he explained to Ed Sutherland in a voice likely heard in Ecuador. That was not a good thing to explain to Ed Sutherland. Ed is a large, grisly man, kind by temperament, but short of temper. And the words spoken by Mr. Brown made him call to mind his beloved and departed mother. So, after thinking it over, and likely remembering his mother's many kindnesses, Ed picked up that old dead goat and started belaboring Mr. C.W. Brown fiercely about the head and shoulders with the carcass.

I have only a shadowy recollection of mouths falling open with shocked sputters and groans. I know that eyes bulged and fists clenched, but nobody made a move toward Ed Sutherland. See, I figure those dearly beloveds gathered there that day had suddenly become Presbyterians. The wild look in Ed Sutherland's eyes and the blur of that goat being used as a weapon helped the people of Epic to grasp that this was, most probably, the preordained plan of the Lord. "All right," we thought, "Thy will be done."

And it was done to the extent that C.W. Brown died two days later.

Looking back, I feel a little sorry for that goat. I expect that not even a *dead* goat would have volunteered to be whomped against C.W. Brown. You could smell that old man a mile away and around the corner. I've heard my dad say that C.W. Brown seemed to suffer no repugnance against a few dead and moldering human bodies, but soap and water seemed to repug him completely. So given a choice, I'd have chosen standing down wind from a dead goat as a pleasant alternative to C.W. Brown. The coroner's report said C.W. Brown died of "excessive abuse by a dead goat." At the inquest it was established (under oath) that Ed Sutherland had been in a foul mood, having suffered a nasty cut to his finger while opening a can of pork and beans on the morning of the incident.

Well, at least in Epic, fair is fair. No charges were filed because almost everyone on the Coroner's jury had, at one time or another, cut their finger on a can of pork and beans. George Blackmore went so far as to tell the assemblage that he, personally, had about given up eating pork and beans because every time he tried he cut his finger. I guess personal testimony carries a good deal of weight. In the end, the jury pretty much agreed that if anybody was to blame for Mr. C.W. Brown's death it was the damn pork and bean people.

2

The dead goat proved to be no problem for me. My dad had heard the whole story at work and was still laughing when he got home. Looking back, I know that my dad was not overly enamored with goatery. He had just hoped to fill my summer and keep me out of reform school.

But the manner of the goat's "passing" had a severe and unpleasant effect on my mom. She announced that she was appalled and disgraced by what had happened and would never be able to show her face in town again. Actually, she screamed, "Never again, never again, never again." And, as if I might need more convincing, she punctuated each "never again" by smashing her aluminum colander against the sink. This is a method of punctuation I have never heard mentioned in school, and I feel that is unfortunate because it is very effective.

"As for you, Wally Eugene Gant," she told me, "You have failed in your responsibility!"

Cripes! I started easing toward the door because when she started her "responsibility" lecture, well, it could go on forever. I guess I would rather have wandered forty years in the wilderness looking back over my shoulder for a passel of pursuing Pharaohs than hear that lecture again.

My mom is a person who can transmigrate from one subject to another with relative ease, so, with the smashed aluminum colander still in her hand, she emphasized me. "I want you to go over to Strang's and get a pint of cream." She flat-out responsibilitized me. "And don't you dare break it."

The Strangs had a small dairy about two blocks from our house and on most days it was one of my responsibilities to fetch milk. We could have just as easily had it delivered, but that summer my mom seemed determined to teach me responsibility. I guess in her mind there weren't many things in this world which would make a boy more responsible than milk.

Mr. Strang spent most of his time either in the barn milking or out on his delivery route in his 1933 Ford panel truck. His wife, Ruby, took care of the drop-in sales at home and pretty much held the hoop for Mr. Strang to jump through.

Ruby Strang is a large woman. My dad said that "Ruby" was a New Orleans name and Ruby was a New Orleans woman. How she ended up in Epic I don't know. My dad said her butt would give West Virginia a run for its money in terms of acreage and square miles. Sometimes, when we were alone together, he would expound on how the balance of power would change in the U. S. Senate if Ruby's butt were granted representation. He never talked about this in front of my mother, because she is not politically inclined.

There was nothing lazy about Ruby. She did her share and more in running the business. Still, she spent a lot of time sitting in an old butt-sprung overstuffed chair.

Mostly she sat there singing Jimmy Rodgers' songs, with an arched-top Harmony guitar teetering on her belly. My dad said her yodeling killed silverfish before they even had a chance to whimper. He said cockroaches, which had endured for millions of years, would turn up their little cockroach toes and just say, "To hell with it."

Ruby's fingers have the length, strength and agility to play in E flat, but her voice is more pleased and more comfortable in the key of G. In those lower tones, you can smell the creosote on the railroad ties, but in E flat, you can almost hear old Ben Dewberry scream as the steam boiler on his train engine explodes.

On the end table beside her chair was a picture of her brother, Howard, with not one stripe on the sleeve of his uniform. He was AWOL from Camp Leonard Wood and had taken two "live" .50 caliber machine gun bullets with him as mementos of his time in service and devotion to his country. Ruby said Howard could have been a General in six months except for the damn bugle horns, which they blew morning, noon, and night. Howard did not care for bugle horns.

I liked Ruby a lot, and if she found me to be a bother, she never let it show. The talk was that on Saturday nights at the tavern she might knock a few heads together, but I'd never seen that side of her.

So I went for the cream and was visiting with Ruby, drinking Kool-Aid, and telling her about the goat peeing on the hearse, when two plain-clothes government men showed up. They had to be government men. The car was almost new and the radiator was not steaming. They were wearing felt hats with the brims turned down. And *suits*! Judas priest!

It was near impossible for Ruby to stop laughing about the goat, but she sobered up when they inquired as to the whereabouts of Howard and the two machine gun bullets. They produced cards and papers and badges. There is no doubt in my mind they could have produced guns. These weren't the first G-men to come looking for Howard. Most folks knew he was hiding out around Strang's place. I sort of saw him lots of times. He had let his black beard grow out so no one would know him. However, since he was the only man in Buffalo County who had a beard, you had to be pretty dumb not to recognize old Howard. Whenever a strange car came along, a sharp eye might spot a beard wafting away into the tall sunflowers west of the railroad track. I would just guess that sunflowers were far and away Howard's favorite flower.

Anyway, Ruby invited the G-men in and offered them a cool glass of rhubarb wine while she pondered the situation. I guess it had been a hot and dusty drive for them because they accepted the wine and looked pleased. Ruby pointed toward the nubbledy-looking couch, and they seemed not to notice the potential for puncture wounds from the sharp coil springs sticking out of the nubbledy.

I saw them spot the two machine gun bullets right off the bat. But I guess the wine was cool and comforting and they likely figured they'd still be paid, whether they were drinking wine or confiscating bullets.

Ruby eased herself into her own chair, and her fat, dimpled hand snaked out and lifted the Harmony guitar from the floor. Her too-red lips inquired if the government men might like to hear a little Jimmy Rodgers. They sipped their wine and thanked her kindly. She, likely with what is called "malice and forethought," cranked the high E string about two-thirds of a tone above what she figured might be acceptable and comfortable for G-men. She tested a couple of chords on the guitar and at the same time motioned with her head that I should refill the G-men's glasses. Prohibition in Kansas or no prohibition in Kansas, when I poured the wine they didn't seem inclined to clap my butt in prison. Kansas law was a Kansas problem.

Ruby pitched the E string still higher and commenced on one of the versions of Jimmy Rodgers' "Blue Yodel." The first verse was about as smooth and pleasant as anything you could ever want to hear. The G-men smiled and raised their glasses at each other. Then, after the part about getting more women than a passenger train could haul, it was time for a yodel. The yodel was my favorite part, but I soon discovered that I had only been exposed to the yodel designed for kids twelve years old and younger. I had never heard Ruby's anti-G-man yodel, and I guess Mr. Roosevelt hadn't either, or the war with the Japs and the Nazis would have been over. No, I am likely misspoken. Mr. Roosevelt was too gentle a man to use such a terrible weapon, even against the Japs and Nazis.

Only God knows what was happening to Ruby's insides as she let out those throat-warpings and gurgles and snarks and wheedles. I disbelieve anybody could do that without damaging their evisceral and pancreas. I wasn't paying much attention to the G-men by then. The most I saw was a sort of blur as they elbowed each other trying to get out the door. Their tires spat gravel back half a block behind them, and they turned onto the main road making a cloud of dust about the size of Nebraska.

Ruby chased them a ways down the driveway, laughing and yodeling at the same time. She had forgotten me and it was past time for me to be home, so I picked up a pint of cream from the big icebox and left. I tried to ignore the ringing in my ears.

Before long I learned that the G-men didn't get far. They slammed into the concrete W.P.A. bridge about a quarter of a mile from Ruby's place. The damage to the bridge was minimal, but the damage to the car and the G-men was maximal. Next day the sheriff questioned Ruby, and then he questioned me. I explained about the yodel as best I could, which was woefully inadequate, and the sheriff said the damn fools should ought to have known better than to try to drive a car after hearing Ruby's version of the "Blue Yodel."

3

Anyway, I got the bottle of cream home without break-ing it, and my dad saw me coming. He kicked the bottom of the screen door because that was the only way to get it open. My mom said, about twenty times a day, "Why don't you just fix that screen door?" and my dad would tell her, "You can't fix a screen door!" The battle of the screen door had gone on forever, like the tides or the sunrise. In our family my dad's word is always law except when my mom starts *her* opinion by saying, "Wilson Gant!" Then my dad will usually say, "By grab, I believe you're right."

My mom took the bottle of cream before I even had a chance to drop it on the floor and pried the cap off to be sure it was good. Then she let out a shriek they likely heard in Decatur County. My dad, who had started to go outside, whirled around and loped back. I guess, hear-ing a sound like that, he wanted to see Mom one more time before she passed on. Mom, without enough breath left in her to speak, just pointed at the bottle.

Dad passed the bottle under his nose and grinned the grin I love to see. After more sips than might be thought necessary to convince himself that it really was not cream, he pronounced that I was the smartest boy he had ever seen. He said he was proud to have me as a son and heir. With the first breath she was able to coup or recoup, Mom declared that I would end up in prison, or turn into Bonnie and Clyde. My dad looked at me and raised his eyebrows, but I thought it was not a good time to question her on how that might come about. At any rate, it was plain to see that she figured any boy sent out for a pint of cream and dumb enough to return with a pint of moonshine whisky did not have a bright future.

Now, likely, I was the only person in Epic who didn't know that the Strangs ran what you might call a "two-pronged" operation. On the one prong, as you might say, was the dairy; on the other prong was a bootleggery.

The moonshine was sold in milk bottles with the outsides painted white. And the trick worked. Maybe only one person in one hundred and twenty-five would have sworn on his mother's grave there was not *milk* in those bottles. The bottle I picked up looked enough like cream to fool me. Still and all, I wasn't expecting to find anything but milk or cream.

Well, I guess I've seen more pleasant looks on the faces of road-smashed turtles than the look my mom adorned on my dad. "Wilson Gant," she told him, "I still need that cream, and I will have no son of mine carrying more of *that* awful stuff back here. You pour it out on the ground and go back with Wally and make sure he gets cream."

My dad kicked the bottom of the screen door and poured just enough drops on the step that my mother could smell and believe she had been obeyed and that the Devil had been foiled again. He put his arm around my shoulder, and we headed up the gravel road toward Strangs'. Every so often he tipped that bottle to his mouth, shook his head in puzzlement, and said, "I'm just not sure if that's cream or not."

Not for the first time I looked at my dad in admiration of his questioning mind. And I'll tell you this: if anyone ever was willing to give a bottle of cream a fair trial, it was my dad.

4

Whether the Strangs were selling moonshine or cream or cream of alligator soup, did not inflect on my jurisdiction. Summer was half over, and I still had a steamboat to build.

In school we had been reading from Mark Twain, and if there was ever anything that sounded more grand than being on a steamboat, I would just be hard put to explain what it might be.

Even a raft like Huck used helping Jim escape would be an elegant thing to have an adventure on, but a real steamboat seemed to be indelibled on my mind.

Purdy Grundy and I had sworn a blood oath that when school let out we would build a steamboat to expedite the escape of the Negro slaves. That the Negro slaves had been freed years and years before we were born did not interfere with the equation. Somewhere in the South there was, undoubtedly, a slave who still had not noticed that he was free. Old Purdy and I burned with abomination. With the help of a steamboat, we intended to dislodge that Negro's misinterpretation.

Mose Washington was a Negro so I guessed his ancestorils had been slaves. He was shy one leg, which he told me was because of a whale. And, while I really wanted to hear how that happened, I somehow felt it would not be polite to ask a Negro about how a whale made off with his leg. What about Jonah? I wondered. Likely Mose just swam a little faster than Jonah.

My mom, who is about as compassionate as anyone who ever came down the pike, told me that Negroes likely had feelings like regular people. And I was not about to injeopardize my friendship with Mose over a leg or a whale. Mose looked to be about one hundred and ninety years old. He was one of my best friends. Pretty often I wheeled my bike up to his porch for a visit, and he was most always in his squeaky old rocker. Almost always, his wife, Mew, who was a voodoo queen, sat beside him. She reminded me of those shepherds in the Bible who kept watch over their flocks by night. Not wishing to belittle in any way, shape, or form the dedication of those shepherds, I will tell you this, Mew would have bitten the head off a snapping turtle to protect Mose.

I know Mose saw me through rheumy, cloudy eyes. Sometimes he would raise or lower his head, trying to make things fit into those eyes again. But I don't guess it ever worked. His face was solemn as granite, but sometimes that old granite would admit to a little fissure, a little granite smile. Best of all, no matter what dumb thing I had on my mind, he never poked fun at me the way most adults did.

So many things in life I needed to ask about: like how my dad and Mose got to be closer than cigarette papers.

I told Mose about Huck Finn and nigger Jim on that raft. And when I told him that Purdy Grundy and I needed to build a steamboat to see if there were any more slaves that needed to be freed, he maybe fissured a little, but not much.

When I tried to talk to my granddad about the steamboat, he purged his understanding of the book of Ecclesiastes through his moustache and told me I was a fool and would likely kill myself. "Vanity of vanities," he told me. "One generation passeth away and another generation cometh. I will hope for more sense from the generation that is cometh-ing."

I suppose wisdom is a fine thing.

Anyway, using an old cane for lift onto his peg-leg, Mose Washington levered himself up and led me through tall foxtail grass to a tarpaper-covered back-yard shed. He trolled around through a length and breadth of long-saved treasures and finally found a half-gallon syrup bucket of bent and rusty nails. "You gonna' build a steamboat," he told me, "You gonna' need a lot of nails." He fished out a short piece of railroad rail which was his anvil and tried to show me how to straighten a bent nail. His eyes just weren't up to it. "Lord," he told me—not a taking of the Lord's name in vain "Lord," but a sad, down-feeling "Lord"—"I can't even see to straighten a nail, but you take these nails and build a steamboat. If I was younger, and if I could see the difference between a nail and an elm tree, I'd build that steamboat right along side of you."

See, that's the way Mose is.

I carried the bucket of nails and followed Mose as he inched and nudged his wooden leg back to the porch. Mew was there waiting; Mew was always there. Tall, skinny as a telegraph pole, eyes that could bore through glass without chipping it. Even with a hair ribbon she couldn't have won a beauty prize in a contest against crocodiles. But she treated me like a piece of gold. She sometimes touched me, lightly. Touched me as she did some of those bright feathers she had all through her house. Bright feathers she told me had come from her home on some island. And sea shells. You wouldn't believe it. She never told me where home had been. Sometimes Mew patted me like I was a puppy, and if I had been predisposed to be a puppy, I would have wanted to be Mew's puppy.

I set the can of nails on the bottom step, and Mose groaned himself into his rocker. Mew handed me a tall lemonade and handed Mose a little cheese glass of what looked like water but made him smile more than water likely would have.

Mose told her that I needed to build a steamboat. Told her why.

If there was any doubt in Mew's mind that there were still a few slaves down South who needed rescuing, it didn't show on her face. It seemed to me that she had a way of seeing things other people couldn't see. She didn't say a word, but the look she gave me might have made flowers bloom.

"But goldarn it," Mose pondered, "It's mighty hard to free slaves without a steamboat! A raft ain't worth sour owl crap when it comes to rescuing slaves, and a steamboat without a whistle plain ain't worth straightening the nails for. I'll think on it."

He tapped his old cane on the porch floor and appealed to his little cheese glass for agreement; then he appealed it back to Mew for a refill.

5

I will tell you this right now: steamboats do not just happen. They do not just spring from the loins of King David, or whoever it was who always seemed to have things springing from his loins.

Once, after Sunday School, I asked my mom when I might expect to have things spring from my loins, and she told me to shut my mouth. So I did.

If I ever have a son I guarantee he will grow up with a full knowledge of loins and springs.

Anyway, the next time I visited Mose, there was a steam whistle lying on the porch. It wasn't a really big steam whistle, but I figured since, likely, Purdy and I didn't have many slaves to rescue, it was big enough. From where or how it came to be there, I never asked and was never told. It was brass, and Mew had polished enough of it to let me know what it could be. What it *should* be, if a fellow was going down a river rescuing.

I expect I grinned like a fool at the sight of that whistle, and Mose snaggle-toothed me a granite-fissure grin back. I guess he knew that slavery had about met its match. Knew that it wouldn't pay to fool around with Wally Eugene Gant. Mew looked as proud as if she had just been crowned Queen of Judeah.

Maybe to keep me from exploding from ecstasy, Mew motioned me to come inside. Mew's house smelled its own smell. Nothing I'd smelled before and nothing I've smelled since has smelled so good. I once heard a fellow say the words "other-worldly" and I'll swear and be damned but that's how Mew's kitchen smelled—other-worldly. The smell of kerosene hung in the air, but that smell hung in most kitchens. Milk has some smell I guess, if only for folks who are hard up for smells. But milk smell was there, too, and the smell of feathers and sea shells. You wouldn't think those bright island-bird-feathers might have a smell, but I know they did. All through the house but especially in the kitchen. Cinnamon, maybe somewhat. Raspberry. Bakey things in the oven; always hot and steamy in that kitchen. A teakettle—spiffing at the back of the stove. I guess that old kettle never had a chance to cool down. This day, the one I'm telling you about, Mew pulled off a chunk of that bakey and dipped some brown goo-stuff over it. Brown sugar, maybe some molasses, maybe a little of what Mose drank from that cheese glass. If heaven is anything like what Mew gave me that day, then heaven is worth striving for.

I took that steam whistle, laid it in my bicycle basket like it was a gift from one of those Magi fellows and started for home. I knew I was the richest boy in Epic!

There are some times in life that stand out special and that evening was one. I leaned my back against the west side of the cistern box and had that old steam whistle across my legs. The moon glinted on it. If there had been a mountain nearby to enhance what was already perfect, I guess I would have pure effervesced.

Next morning I had another thought. It came from that sun-sparkledy spot Mew had polished on the steam whistle. I wanted to show that whistle to Ruby. Some people understand things and some people don't. There was no doubt in my mind Ruby would understand.

I knew from my dad that Ruby was from New Orleans. New Orleans is down where they had slaves, and I needed some advice concerning slaves. I pushed my bicycle up the last part, the steep part, of the rough cinder driveway. The driveway, and mostly all the rest of the place was also covered with bits of fresh water clam shells, the scraps of buttons from Epic's old button factory. Button scraps which had been put there to make the chickens smile, and the chickens had been put there because Ruby's old, red, hollow-tile house had once been a hatchery. A place where chickens could calmly lay eggs, beget more chickens, and smile at the abundance of button parts. But that was back, away back. Sometimes my dad seemed to bemoan the fact that I could not remember when "away back" was. See, picture him, drawing on his cigarette, flicking it away toward the raspberry bushes, and saying, "but that was before the market crash, that was before the goddamn Japs bombed Pearl Harbor, that was when hens still appreciated fresh-water clam shell button pieces. That was before the world went to hell in a hand basket." Then he would walk away, and I would follow, toward the kitchen. Toward where my mom would offer her best: split down the middle fried weenies. I'll swear nobody can fry weenies like my mom.

The day was already hot and I was sweaty. Little dog-pecker gnats pestered the back of my neck and under my arms. My encroachment upon Ruby and Mr. Strang's property was announced by a cedar-tree-living crow. It lived east, east of the hollow-red-tile house where Ruby lived. "Crumbled" is what you might call the far end of that poor old building. Discouragement sloping into near nothingness.

That old black crow had assumed the responsibility of guarding the place, and you couldn't get within a block but what you were spotted and announced. She'd bad-mouth that crow when he was around. But when she knew it wasn't within hearing distance, Ruby swore the crow was worth more than nine watchdogs put together.

Most days she would set out a tuna can with a little Moon Butter in it as a sort of payment. When its belly was full and the crow took off, you could tell the exact time the Moon Butter kicked in and started working its magic. That old crow would sometimes forget to flap its wings, would seem to look around and wonder how in the world it came to be away up in the air. When it finally recognized the tree it called home, the easy part was over. The landing was what you might call trial and error. Mostly the first few tries were error. Sometimes it zoomed away off to the left, next time maybe closer but a little to the right. When it finally got perched, it would let out a loud shriek to let the world know there were damn few things a crow couldn't handle. A drunk crow is far and away more fun than all the goats in Buffalo County.

I need to tell you about Moon Butter—still and all, I don't know much about Moon Butter. Ruby made Moon Butter and Ruby sold Moon Butter, but Ruby didn't *talk* about Moon Butter. The only person on God's green earth who had the recipe for Moon Butter was Ruby. I've heard that God knows everything, but if God had the recipe for Moon Butter, I would be very much surprised. See, here's the way I figure it, if God had had a Moon Butter route, He wouldn't have had time to invent the planet Pluto, or tigers, or pocket knives. See, likely

God was proud that he had created Ruby and proud that Ruby had invented Moon Butter. But, the fact remains, it was Ruby, not God, who had the market for Moon Butter in all the Little Balkans. Folks who didn't crave Moon Butter were few and far between.

I didn't need to knock. Ruby was standing there laughing and filling the doorway. My mom would have shuddered and passed peach seeds if she knew how much I liked Ruby.

I told Ruby about my plan. I told her about how somewhere down south there was likely a slave in a rotten old canebrake, a snaky old canebrake, being forced to break his fingers breaking cane. Ruby looked at me as if I were an askance and said that such a thing seemed mean and likely despicable. She said that her daddy's mom had used a cane, and had anybody ever tried to break her daddy's mom's cane, she would have flat sautéed his gizzard. Ruby is not one to mince words. And, as she is from New Orleans, not Epic, she weren't about to simply fry a gizzard. She would flat sauté the dang thing. I just guess if there is anything in the world worse than having your gizzard sautéed I would be hard put to say what it might be.

I told her that Mose Washington had given me a bucket of bent nails and showed me how to straighten them. Then I pulled out my gunnysack and uncovered the steam whistle.

Ruby blinked, somewhat, and finally admitted that that was the finest steam whistle she had ever seen. Getting her enthusiasm under control after a while, she finally allowed as how I was the luckiest boy in Epic, having both a bucket of bent nails and a steam whistle.

Then I remembered that I hadn't yet told her about old Huck Finn and nigger Jim, nor how Purdy Grundy and I figured to build a steamboat before school started and free whatever slaves remained. I asked her opinion as to how many slaves might still need to be freed down there in the South. She scratched her neck and fanned away those gnats, which did not fan away to any great extent, then allowed that for sure there were a bunch of worthless Darkies down there, but she didn't recollect seeing any slaves.

Ruby's eyes were large and brown and deep as forever. They didn't miss much either. Now, you've got to understand about Ruby and me. And I don't know how it came about, but if I had been a gnat on Ruby's nose, and she knew it was me biting, she wouldn't have squashed me. I think about Ruby and I know she wouldn't have squashed me.

Inside, she picked up that old Harmony guitar, and offered a soft G7. That's when I noticed the photograph of her brother, Howard. It had been changed, altered, enthused upward. No longer did those sleeves beg for a stripe or two. No, sir, a purple Crayola had added more stars to his shoulders than you would find in the entire constellation of Amphibious. His mouth seemed to be clunched down on the stem of a corncob pipe, and if there was one Jap soldier in a hundred and twenty-five who could have told the difference between Howard and General McArthur, I will just kiss Harry Rooney's left-handed sister's spotted cat's ass.

Those big brown eyes must have seen the downtrodden in my face, because she strummed again and looked thoughtful. "You know," she said, "the more I think about it, I maybe do seem to remember seeing a couple of slaves south of town." She dipped her fingers down into what might be rightly called her "cleavage," but which was also the cash register of the two-pronged Strang dairy and bootleggery. She gave me a smile which glimmered gold at the side of one tooth, fished out a one dollar bill and laid it in my hand. Nearly more money than I had ever had at one time in my life.

"Use this," she said, "to help build your steamboat. It's a cry and a shame for people to be forced to break their mama's cane. And her smile was all golden—pure gold.

6

People say that honesty is the best policy, and sometimes it likely is. So I guess I am obliged to tell you that although Purdy Grundy was my best friend, he was also a sort of Fred Astaire when it came to building a steamboat. He danced around a lot, but he didn't straighten an appreciable of nails. My dad, on the other hand, was a champion nail straightener. Not every evening, but a lot of evenings, we would sit there by the cistern, on that roundabout concrete, straightening nails.

We talked, and he was always honest with me. I asked him if he believed there were still slaves that needed to be freed down there in the south. He looked at me ponder-eyed, and said, "Yes, likely there is, back there somewhere in the canebrakes."

In all honesty, I wouldn't have known a canebrake if one crashed through the screen door and bit me on the neck. This seemed as good a time as any to confess my ignorance, so I flat out asked what a canebrake was. It was a poor time to ask. He had hit a nail a little slanchwise and stung his fingers. Nail-straightening-stung fingers are every bit as bad as splinters. Maybe worse. "A canebrake," he told me, standing and slapping the dust off the backside of his trousers, "A canebrake is a place where they break cane! Judas Priest! What grade are you in?"

That whistle. That whistle is what caught Purdy's interest. I guess he could see himself standing up straight in the pilothouse, pulling that rope, tooting that dang whistle. More fun than straightening nails. That bothered me because I knew I couldn't build a steamboat by myself. My dad was walking toward the house so I hollered him back. He turned against the wind and lit a Camel, rubbing his nail-stung fingers together. I told him about Purdy and the whistle. I told him I couldn't build a damn steamboat by myself, and he didn't even tell me not to say "damn." My mom would have crucified me, dead, and buried!

He squatted there beside me, thinking, and let the smoke from his Camel escape through his nose. "Don't be too hard on Purdy," he told me. We sat there, staring at nothing except grass and dandelions.

"When I rule the world," he said, "there will be a steam whistle in every town, right there in the middle of the town square. That way, when a fellow feels the need, he can just walk up and pull the rope. That old whistle will ease his mind and placate his liver. Then he can get back to straightening whatever nails life gives him to straighten. And there won't be anymore wars!" He nodded, confirming his agreement with himself. "And, we won't need any more preachers. The aches and woes of the world will just vanish into oblivion. Everybody needs a steam whistle from time to time. It'll be a noisier but a better world."

Pleased with himself, he determined toward the house sucking his nail-stung finger, already transangulating how many feet south the courthouse would need to be moved to get the steam whistle in the exact center of the square.

Ciphering the cost of the steam boiler and a fellow to operate it, composing his speech to the County Commissioners to explain the need, he picked up speed as he neared the back door. "Mother," he bellowed, "We've got to move the courthouse!"

I knew she wouldn't bother much listening about courthouses or Commissioners or steam whistles. She was preparing her preeminent dish: fried, split weenies, embroidered on a bed of fried potatoes, with grape Jell-O served in the little bowls her grandma had brought from Kentucky.

No. Without looking up, she would just tell him to go fix the screen door.

7

Just north of the railroad-tie cowshed my dad had built was what we called the "hay barn." It wasn't much more than a shed itself. There was a place for pigeons under the roof, but if anyone in Epic ever saw a pigeon there, I never heard of it. Lots of evenings I climbed to the top. That old roof groaned under me. I climbed up there with malice and forethought, because I hoped that someday Miss Maudie and Edmond Denny from WIBW would take a mis-turn off the highway, hear me singing, and invite me to be on the radio with them. I expect lots of people heard me singing on those evenings. "Carry Me Back to Old Virginny" was my best song. In my opinion my singing was pretty good. In my dad's opinion, well, he said he was glad we no longer had a cow because I likely would have curdled the milk.

One evening I had just got to the part where "that's where the cotton and the corn and 'taters grow," and I'd hunched up my breath for "the birds warbling sweet in the springtime" when a car *did* pull into the driveway. It

wasn't Miss Maudie and Edmond Denny, though. It was
Mr. Strang..

Mr. Strang was older than God's wheelbarrow and
looked to have more miles on him. You could tell by looking that every move pained him. He'd come to hire me to
be his legs. It had to be Ruby's idea. She liked me and
knew I could keep my mouth shut.

My mom hollered me down from the roof of the barn
when Mr. Strang asked for me. He offered me fifty cents
a week to ride with him every day to help make deliveries. I looked at my mom for her consent.

Now, see, my mom likely knew that the Strangs ped-
dled a little booze, but the thought of my being in the
close approximation of milk wavered her mind. To her,
milk would be my salvation and teach me responsibility.
To me, the fifty cents a week would buy parts needed for
the steamboat. My soul and body! Fifty cents a week
could buy me a wristwatch. It could buy me, in time, an
electric motor!

That evening I lay on my belly and searched the cata-
logue for the things I might buy. I lay there
belly-dreaming. I lay there thinking about old Purdy
Grundy saying, "Wally, could you lend me the borrow of
a nickel?" I would smile at him, because I was rich, and
if a fellow is rich it's easy to smile. "Purdy," I would say,
"here is fifteen cents. God speed, and blest be the tie that
binds."

And old Purdy's mouth would drop open and he would
say, "Wally, I didn't know you could talk Bible!"

"Hell, yes," I would tell him. "I make fifty cents a week!"

I was too covered with barn-roof grunge to go with Mr.
Strang that afternoon. But the next day when I walked
over to the dairy, I was shiny as a school teacher's apple.
I was plenty glad I looked sparkling too. When Mr.
Strang made his deliveries, he didn't look like a dairy

farmer. No, sir, he wore a bow tie, checkeredy socks and a plaid, lightweight, seersucker wrinkledy coat. His pants had wide stripes and, I'll tell you, he looked more like a tenor banjo player than a milkman. He looked me up and down pretty close to see if I looked adequate to represent the Strang dairy business. Satisfied that my appearance wouldn't curdle the milk, he let me get in the truck. I tried to sit straight and look as if I had had fifty-one jobs before this one.

The truck was already loaded on the first day of my new job, but afterwards I would walk over to the dairy and help him load. Mr. Strang wasn't normally much of a talker; however, on this first day, he had quite a bit to say. He told me that my job would be to carry the milk into the homes and businesses, which I already knew. Then he said, "Now son, I want you to understand that the dairy business is a hard business to stay in. There are a lot of people who would like to have what Ruby and me have successfully built over the years. They'd give their damned ears to learn the secrets of our success. But we don't tell them. Yes, sir, they'd give their damned ears! And *you* must not tell anything either. Ruby said you was a boy who could be trusted. We're trusting you not to tell anybody anything about our dairy business. Anybody asks you anything, you just tell them you don't know. Tell them you just carry in the milk."

I'll swear I was confused. It appeared to me that anybody who had a cow and a milk bottle could sell milk. Still and all, the idea of being in on secrets appealed to me mightily. He waited, then looked at me as if he had asked a question. I alerted and told him I would never, ever, tell anybody any damned thing at all about the dairy business. He looked at me again, this time with a weak smile. I guess he hadn't realized that I was man enough to swear.

But then he looked at me again, and he wasn't smiling. He said, "I know you heard what Ruby called me this afternoon." He slipped out from his belt the most glittery wicked knife you ever dreamed of, and said, "You ever mention that to anyone in this world, and I will cut off your water tower!"

I was not completely sure what my water tower might be, but I was darn sure, if I had one, I didn't want it cut off. Not for this. Not for what I had heard Ruby holler out to him. She'd said, "Hey, lover-belly honey-toes, stop in here a couple minutes before you go."

Whatever she had in mind for lover-belly honey-toes, I was darn sure it was not as important as my water tower; so I told him I hadn't heard a thing.

That first day it seemed like we stopped at about every house in town. I carried the milk in, sometimes leaving it on the front porch and sometimes leaving it in a screened-in back porch. Some places I was supposed to open the back door and put the milk in the icebox. That felt strange, going into someone's house, but I got used to it. What I never got used to was the cockroaches. I sure as heck was not afraid of cockroaches. But there they were, in about every backdoor place I went. Even in Jesse Kliegman's home, for cripes sake! And who would have thought that? Mr. Kliegman was known far and wide as the only honest state legislator to ever come out of Buffalo County. My dad voted for him every time votes seemed appropriate, even as a write-in vote after Mr. Kliegman got put in prison. My dad maintained that Mr. Kliegman never in his life did anything illegal. He just happened to own a piece of land that the new highway suddenly and inexplicably went four miles out of its way to make a bend through. "The Buffalo County Bend," it was called. My dad said the road completely ruined Mr. Kliegman's perfectly good wheat field, (and just because some politicians wanted folks to be able to enjoy the vast expanse of yellow limestone rocks which covered almost every inch of it).

At some places, Mr. Strang pointed to a separate batch of milk bottles and told me to deliver one, two, or three of those. Wasn't my place to ask questions. Milk looked like milk to me. But it weren't—not always.

Now, I told you that the Strang Dairy was a two-pronged operation. To wit and theretofore: milk and moonshine. Well, it didn't take me long to learn that it was really a *three*-prong operation. I can tell you without fear of contraception, that it was the third prong that made the business go. It was the third prong which kept the Big Boy bootleggers in Buffalo County from just wiping Ruby's little old bootleggery off the map. It was the third prong that paid my fifty cents a week. It was the third prong for which some people would have pulled out their grandma's toenails to get the recipe. The third prong was Ruby's Moon Butter.

In my conceit I'd like to believe I was about as close to Ruby and as trusted by Ruby as anyone. We shelled peas together. We snapped beans together. Sometimes we sang Jimmy Rodgers' songs together, and Ruby tried in the most sincere way to teach me to yodel. It was wasted effort, because my body was not built for the stress of yodeling. And my mom's ears were not built for the stress of listening to me practice.

Now, I felt free to come and go as I pleased at Ruby's. I knew where the Kool-Aid was, and I knew I was welcome to dipper myself some whenever I wanted. I was at home at Ruby's. But there was one room in that rambling old stretched out place to which I was never invited. That was the room where Ruby made her Moon Butter. There weren't a soul in the world that knew the secret of Ruby's Moon Butter. There was not a soul, except Ruby, who knew how to make it. Not even Mr. Strang.

No, sir, if Ruby ever died, Moon Butter would die with her. And the world of Buffalo County would near collapse. My dad told me that at least three of the founding mothers of the Buffalo County Women's Christian Temperance Union would prefer death to the thought of life without Moon Butter. Women who would rather suck a red hot poker than taste alcohol wouldn't see much point in living without biscuits slathered with Moon Butter and raspberry jelly. They would just perish away.

8

Afternoons, after all the local deliveries were made, Mr. Strang turned the truck south toward Armageddon. By my standards a large town, Armageddon has some fine, big brick homes. You could stack a good portion of the buildings in Epic end on end and still not reach the height of some of those downtown buildings.

We drove right on through the fancy part. We drove to where there wasn't much except tarpaper-roll-brick-covered houses. Armageddon lay about eleven miles south of Epic. Still in Buffalo County, but barely. If a fellow ever needed to try to explain the "Little Balkans," I don't guess he could have done much better than to give the explainee a tour of the bad part of Armageddon. Like a lot of what is called the "Little Balkans," the countryside was raw-scrapped and ugly. Let me say it this way, if you were walking through a pasture that might contain little piles of Armageddons, you would want to be pretty careful where you stepped your foot down.

My dad claimed that in better days, that particular end of Armageddon had boasted a Catholic church and a jail, but the citizens kept stealing them so the fad of replacing them sort of faded out. Some of the folks in Armagedden were friskier than a sack full of weasels. It was mostly enpopulated by people who distilled alcohol and sold it and drank it. Which is why Mr. Strang always stopped his truck in the back of a tavern owned by Mr. Booger Red Passeggiata. Mr. Booger Red's Emporium stood at the intersection of Ninth Street and Perdition Boulevard.

Of course, Booger Red was not his Christian name. Booger Red's father had embarrassed the whole Italian community by marrying a beautiful redheaded Irish girl. The result was Booger Red.

Why, no new mama in the world would cuddle her precious little bundle to her bosom and proclaim, "By grab, we'll call this one Booger Red!" No, sir, Booger's mom did her bosom-cuddling and her proclaiming and announced that this one would be called "Pearl LaVern Passeggiata."

Now, dig back into the history of Egypt, or even Milwaukee, and I doubt you will find a greater sin than that. The pharaohs and the King Harrods and, some would say, the Roosevelts, might, likely, feel like hanging back towards the end of the line on judgment day. See, what they *should* do would be try to get right behind Booger Red's mother. The way I see it is like this: when Saint Peter hears that she named her *son* Pearl LaVern Passeggiata, the next thirty or so people would just be waved on in without preamble or *ad valorem*. They could just file by, unmolested, because Saint Peter would be on the phone to old Satan inquiring if any provision had been made for such a wicked person as Pearl LaVern's mother. I can see Satan dabbing at his scorched eyebrow, wiping the sweat away, and saying, "Jesus Christ, Pearl LaVern Passeggiata?"

And then, Saint Peter would say, "I've told you before, don't take the Lord's name in vain!"

And then, Satan would say, "Well, I've got a spare bedroom, but it would cost a fortune to add the fire bricks and get it ready, and times are hard right now."

And then Saint Peter would say, "I don't recollect anybody saying it was going to be cheap or easy to run Hell."

And then, Satan would slam the receiver down, and the last thing Saint Peter would hear would be something about trying for another bond issue.

Howsoever, just walk around Armageddon and it was pretty easy to spot the fellows who had found humor in calling Booger Red by his Christian name. They were the ones with the slanch-wise noses and the mostly bit-off ears.

We stopped at Booger Red's because that's where Ruby bought most of the booze for her bootleggery. That booze was also the main ingredient for Ruby's Moon Butter. And I guess the business transaction was about a trade off. About as much booze going into the truck as there was Moon Butter coming out. Nobody bought more Moon Butter than Booger Red.

Mr. Strang motioned me back and told me that Booger Red had no use in this rosy, blue-eyed world for kids. He said he would go in first and explain that I was a special friend of Ruby's and carried my weight in the business. And I knew to keep my mouth shut tighter than a bull's ass in fly time.

Booger Red loomed there. Just loomed. I don't know if I felt more like the Titanic or the iceberg. But, if you have never been loomed at by Booger Red, then you have never been appreciably loomed. Booger Red was seven feet tall. Maybe nine, maybe eleven. It didn't really matter. By the look in his eyes I knew that my head was about to be plucked from my body. Mr. Strang did the introductions, and it was a waste of time. A life-time of my mom's teaching of politeness and gentility was gone, just gone. What I saw was a mean-looking, maybe evil, eleven-foot-tall piece of mankind with red hairs growing out of it. What he saw was likely a septic tank which had lost its will to function as one might hope.

I should have said something like "I am pleased to make your acquaintance, Mr. Red." But I didn't. I just stood with my mouth open—and farted.

9

Now, see, I have never read that book written by the famous lady who proclaims about etiquette. I sometimes wish I had, because there is a feeling of inadequacy that comes with not knowing which fork to use with the clam bisque. Still and all, I wonder did she include a chapter dealing with those occasions when breaking wind smoothed and balmed the way to social acceptance? I doubt it. Which just goes to prove that we are never too old to learn.

But with that little embarrassment of mine, Booger Red just flat melted, like a stuck-in-the-pocket saved-until-later Hershey bar. He grinned. Maybe his first grin since Armistice Day 1918. We unloaded the Moon Butter and loaded the booze. Maybe it took fifteen minutes and, all the while, Booger Red had me in the corner of his eye; watching, wrinkled-browed, considering. Mr. Strang gentled his sore bones into the truck and was ready to strike for home. But then, Booger Red laid his hand on my shoulder. It was not at all hurtful or anything like that. No, sir, it gave me a grinning feeling. He

walked me right down the middle of Perdition
Boulevard. I knew there were people seeing. At first I
had the eye-blink thought that this must be how a goat
feels, being led around. Then I thought, no, this is how
the Crown Prince of Austro-Hungaria feels. Or maybe
old Abraham, getting perambulated through the streets
of ancient Asertainia by the hand of some king with a
name embracing a lot of "z's" and "h's" with a "j" at the
end. I reached up and took hold of his knuckle-busted
hand and knew, most deep, that after today I could walk
down the worst street of Armageddon in the far dark
side of midnight and not have my throat cut.

Back in the truck and heading for home, there was a
different feeling. The windows were rolled down, of
course, but it wasn't just the fresh air and it wasn't the
sneezy goldenrod blowing in that made the difference.

And it wasn't me. I hadn't grown any taller or any
heavier or, likely, any handsomer. Maybe, just a little
smarter. I figured it over in my mind. Booger Red had
accepted me.

It wasn't me that had changed; it was Mr. Strang. He
looked at me proud, a little puffed up and more happy
than he had been earlier.

Seven miles back north of Armageddon, Mr. Strang
turned east toward Galenaville. If you aspire to be
Napoleon and conquer the world then you had just as
well spare yourself from going three miles east over to
Galenaville and then three miles back going west to the
highway. Because Galenaville, conquer-wise, does not
offer a great deal to be aspirated.

The town was a lot like Armageddon but, somehow,
lacking that warmth and beauty I had not even noticed
in Armageddon. We stopped at Galenaville because of a
fellow named Mike O'Riley who was the local distribu-
tor of Moon Butter. Mike O'Riley was as dissimilar to

his name as was Pearl LaVern Passeggiata. Mike O'Riley had flat been misdenomered. With a name like Mike O'Riley, a fellow ought to be able to twist the end off an ax handle with his bare hands, but this Mike O'Riley was a mouse of a man. A blustery runt with a rodent's face but, maybe, a runt with sharp teeth. If he had been to Sunday School in the last three months, I would be very much surprised. But, at that time, Mr. Strang was not in the mood to fool with a runt mouse who hadn't been to Sunday School; maybe not even in the mood to take much sass from a cyclone. That's where the difference came in. The difference I was telling you about that I noticed in the truck. Booger Red's acceptance of me seemed to provoke about a modicum of new respect in my direction.

When Mike O'Riley glowered at me for the transgression of being a kid, Mr. Strang bellied up in his tenor-banjo-player striped pants, like he would as soon as not bite the spare tire off a Chevrolet and laid the word on Mike O'Riley: I was a friend of Ruby's and had been hand-on-the-shoulder walked through the bad part of Armageddon by Booger Red himself.

Well, Mike O'Riley seemed to have an immediate re-evaluation of our relationship. Don't get me wrong, I was in no way, shape, or form just malfunctioning under the misapprehension that I amounted to anything at all in God's green world. It was the words "Ruby," and, even more, "Booger Red," that gave me my aura. I will tell you this: Mike O' Riley might have been a mouse, but he was smart enough to know that Booger Red was the Big Cheese in the Little Balkans.

I helped Mr. O'Riley stack the Moon Butter on a block of ice in the ice box, and Mr. Strang spun the tires as we made our bows and left. If Ruby had seen that, she would have for sure bawled him out for wasting rubber while our brave boys were fighting and dying in unseemly places for lack of rubber. But, if ever I saw a man who had an imaginary pearl-handled revolver in his belt, it was Mr. Strang.

On the way home Mr. Strang was whistling "Bye Bye Blackbird" with such desecration that I figured every blackbird in Buffalo County would be lining up at the courthouse to be reconfigured into a robin. The wind sort of whiffled in around the windshield and I sat back and gave thought to names. Somehow they didn't seem to match with reality. Booger Red, for instance, shouldn't have been named Pearl LaVern Passeggiata. And Mike O'Riley? That was just a cry and a shame.

But I, who have been classified by some as one of "the least of these my brethren," was in no position to cast the first stone. According to my dad, on the day of my birth, Dr. Hilton slapped my butt to such an extent that I would have never chosen, given the choice, to live in a world where people did things like that to a newcomer. I don't remember being in a hurry to emerge anyway. Given the choice and knowing what I soon learned about this world, I would have said, "Wait, now. Let's just think about this a minute."

I may have mentioned earlier my enthralling singing voice. Those in attendance at my birth will affirm that that proclivity was not immediately noticed. My dad told me that my squalling had been so awful that, had Dr. Hilton not had another call to make, he, (my dad) would have sent me back.

Likely eager to be rid of me, Dr. Hilton laid me at my mother's bosom to be nourished and named. Now see, there is no reason to doubt that my mom had had a hard day. And, in all honesty, I will have to admit that my screaming gave no promise that her life might improve in the next twenty years. She was distraught. And when

Dr. Hilton asked what name he should inscribe on the birth certificate, she proclaimed, "Walnut! Walnut Eugene Gant."

"Walnut Eugene Gant? No! Judas Priest!" Dr. Hilton told her.

"No," my mom said. (It was never easy to change my mom's mind.) "Judas Priest might be a good name for some boys, but he doesn't seem like a Judas Priest." She looked at my wrinkledy face and agreed with herself, "Walnut Eugene Gant!"

At that point my dad had braved his way into the birthing room and was standing about three feet south of proximity. So he heard most of the conversation, at least the Walnut Eugene Gant part. "Judas Priest!" my dad echoed in full agreement with the Doctor.

It was at about that point that my mom slipped into restful, peaceful oblivion. Dr. Hilton lowered his head and said he was sorry not to be able to oblige the wishes of the Mrs., but part of his sworn Hypercritical oath was to never allow a child to be named "Walnut."

I guess in all the world there was never a man who had more respect for the Hypercritical oath than my dad. So, together, they conspired and entered my name as Wally. "Wally Eugene Gant."

10

I didn't tell my mom about the afternoon I had just experienced. No, sir, I had learned, long before, the truth of that old saying: Ignorance is bliss. I had learned that the more ignorant my mom was about my comings and goings the more blissful I was likely to remain.

And she didn't ask me much that day. She *did* ask if Mrs. Porter's icebox was clean when I put the milk in. I told her, "No, Ma'am, it surely was not. There was a dead mouse lying right there partly on top of a carrot. It was cold and stiff and had been gnawing on her vegetables."

She gasped and said, "Good Lord almighty! I am not surprised!" She couldn't have been more pleased had I told her I had found three silver dollars.

Of course, there was no dead mouse in Mrs. Porter's icebox, and I knew it was a mean and ornery thing to say. But, to her credit, my mom had an inquiring mind, especially about her neighbors. And, if I needed to invent a dead mouse or a few cockroaches to brighten her day, her happiness made it worth the effort.

But that day she did not have time to question me closely. Nor did she let me into the kitchen. See, I was not supposed to know that she was making a cake for tomorrow—for my thirteenth birthday, for gosh sakes. Like I had not had that on my mind for the last month! Like I had not lain awake, night after night, imagining the joy I would engender should I receive my own silver B-flat cornet! Goodness knows I had dropped a few subtle hints about how proud a mother and father might be to see their own son marching in the Fourth of July parade playing a silver B-flat cornet.

Now, contrary to what some folks might say, I had not survived for thirteen years on this old earth by being stupid. So I gave Mom my biggest smile and did my best to assume the innocence of a blind orphan. I told her I guessed I would go out and straighten a few nails for the steamboat. You would not believe how happy that seemed to make her. She said she would give me a penny apiece for every nail I straightened before supper. I had the feeling that had I told her I was going out and eat wooly worms I could have gotten a penny apiece for them, too.

It's not easy going to sleep when you know that the next time you see daylight you will be thirteen years old. It is ten times harder going to sleep hoping that when you wake you will find a silver B-flat cornet beside your bed. Hoping that in about two weeks, on the Fourth of July, you would be marching down Main Street blowing out sweet music and dressed in a uniform that would put the King of Prussia to shame. Knowing that people would be whispering, "My soul and body, who would have ever thought the Gant boy could ever do anything like that?"

Well, day broke and with it broke my most precious dreams. There was no silver B-flat cornet. There *was* a package from my grandfolks, which contained a billfold embossed with a picture of a *rose* and with a dollar bill in it. I knew that sooner or later I would have to write a thank you note telling them that I had spent most of my adult life wishing for a damn, dingle-brained, sissy, damn, double-damn, sissy, sissy, sissy quadruple-damn billfold with a puke picture of a rose on it.

On the heels of that wonderment, my mom presented me with such a multitude of socks and underpants—enough—enough that I could finally relax. No longer would I toss and turn at night, wondering where my next double-dingle-brained damn pair of underpants would come from.

As soon as I could, I excused myself with all the aplomb and adroitment possible and went to the cellar. It was a good place to ponder the whopper-skewed joys of being thirteen years of age!

I did find some comfort in that cellar. I utilized all the words I had heard my father use while repairing the transmission of our Model T Ford. I had used them before in dealing with our goats. And, in all modesty, I will admit that in using those words I had. long since ceased being an amateur. In all honesty, if those goats had any doubt about my feelings toward them, their parents, their grandparents, and their how-some-ever assorted ancestors clear back to the book of Ecclesiastes, I would be very much surprised.

Then I noticed two jars of my mom's pickled beets on the shelf. Smirking, dingle-brained pickled beets are the worst kind. They knew I had not received a silver B-flat cornet for my birthday, and they were rubbing my nose in it. Now, you may say what you want about me, but you can never, honestly, say that Wally Eugene Gant ever put up with any smirks from any pickled-damn-dingle-brain beets. I smashed them on the floor and felt some better.

At the dairy, Mr. Strang and Ruby give me two dollars and wished me many happy returns of the day. Nevertheless, I went to bed that night feeling pretty glum.

Well, morning came—as I was afraid it would.

I woke knowing I owned the world's largest collection of underpants and a billfold with a rose on it and I likely would be called on to explain the sudden demise of two jars of pickled beets.

First off the bat my mom put me to work weeding the garden. She told me I had to spend a half-hour doing that, and then I should take care of the goats. It was slavery, pure and simple. I could only be thankful that we didn't have any cane to break. If ever anyone felt the burden of remorse, it was me. The yoke of guilt was on my neck because lately I had been too lazy to straighten more nails to build a steamboat to free my brother slaves. And, I will tell you this: if ever anybody had achieved a deeper understanding concerning the painful and brutal meaning of "woe betide" slavery than Wally Eugene Gant, I would be very much surprised.

Now see, I had not spent three-quarters of my life in a "Don't-you-dare-scratch," butt-numbing church pew, without learning a modicum of Christian theology. "Woe betide!" That's what I mostly learned. And "woe betide" was the exact way I felt as I started toward my fourteenth birthday without a silver B-flat cornet.

But it wasn't until my dad came home from work the second day that I learned what happiness was.

Dad came in carrying a big package and wearing a smile eight feet wide. They were both for me. When I tore into that package I immediately rued my blasphemous tongue and my rudeness to pickled beets.

There it was! The most beautiful thing I had ever laid eyes on. In a shiny black case with a soft, purple lining. There it actually was, my own silver B-flat cornet! I was almost too awestruck to touch it. It sparkled more than all the stars in the constellation of Onomatopoeia. Of course, I did touch it. All the wild horses in the world—had they been inclined to keep a boy from touching his B-flat cornet—could not have kept me from touching it.

I slipped the mouthpiece into the mouthpiece end and gave out with a blast that would have made Shakespeare himself weep with envy. My mom and dad looked at each other. Just looked at each other. Then they looked back at me. And then they looked at each other again. I could tell that their hearts were bursting with pride; they were likely asking themselves why in the world they hadn't bought me a silver B-flat cornet sooner.

The next day, after my milk route, I carried my new horn over to Miss Brownlow's for my first lesson. She worked the valves up and down a few times and announced my cornet to be a fine instrument. Then she asked me if I had made a sound on it yet. I maintained my modesty enough to just say "Yes."

Well, sir, to prove my point, I lifted that good old silver B-flat cornet to my lips and flat-out showed her what a talented thirteen year boy could do. Had I made a *sound* on it yet? I should hope to tell you! Maybe never so fine before, maybe never so loud before, as the sound I made then for Miss Brownlow. I would be less than honest if I did not admit that I got her attention. I had heard of folks being in a state of bliss, but I had not, hithertofore, witnessed bliss in the flesh until I saw Miss Brownlow's eyes roll right up into her head. I wanted to get off on my best foot, so, at the risk of endangering my health, I maintained that sound until my breath was completely gone.

It took her a long time to pull herself back together, but I will give her credit for doing her best. She was obviously having trouble keeping back the tears. Finally, she told me that she had worked with a lot of beginning students, but she had never worked with anyone as beginning as me.

She dismissed me early, which showed me that she had a good heart, and I went home and straightened thirteen nails in remembrance of my fellow slaves.

11

I expect it had not been much more than half an hour after Mr. Strang dropped me off home, having finished our afternoon deliveries, when he was back again. Well, "back" doesn't do justice to the fact. He roared that truck in and slid the tires.

Ruby was in the seat beside him and, from the look on her face, I judged that there might be maybe three alligators in the world who would risk crossing her path. And they would be those whom we call "mentally deficient."

Ruby stared straight ahead, her jaws clenched. I knew something was dead wrong; but since the windshield had not yet shattered, I figured the world had not ended. On the other hand, I could feel that the world might be *about* to end. So I checked the buttons on my fly because I did not want to meet St. Peter for the first time while committing an indiscretion.

Mr. Strang moved faster than I would have believed possible. Moved himself from the truck and talked to my mom. He explained that there was a lot of work needed done at the dairy and they would appreciate the extra use of my help. He said it would be even better and more simple if I could just spend the night at their place and work the next day.

Now, I will tell you this: there was likely never a mom who graced this earth who was more generous than my mom.

It must have been a wrench to her heart to face having me gone, but she was never one to deny a person in need. She told Mr. Strang to keep me as long as was necessary, but she would be pleased to have me back for Thanksgiving. She didn't come right out and say it, but she kind of left it hanging in the air that she would take it as a personal favor if I could at least be home for Christmas.

I squatted in the back, behind Mr. Strang and Ruby, and we were off like a shooting star.

Ruby didn't say a word for a mile or two. She just watched that windshield as if it might make a break for freedom. Finally, she reached an inviting hand back over her shoulder and I took it. Ruby's hand was like the rest of her, aplenty. She squeezed my hand, and I could feel the used-to-be-painted fingernails bite in. She said, "Wally, Booger Red's been shot. Shot in the goddamned back! It was that Chicago bunch. They've been prowling around. They ain't satisfied just hauling our fine Deep Shaft moonshine back East. They want to take over the whole works. They want my Moon Butter, too. Likely I'll be shot next. I need you with me."

Now, see, it's one thing to be thirteen years old. It's one thing to receive a billfold with a rose on it. It's one thing, even, to have a silver B-flat cornet. It's a complete other thing to have someone say they need you.

It was far and away better than any blessing of God I had so far received, to squat in the back of the Strang

Dairy panel truck, holding Ruby's squeezing hand, headed south toward the Sisters of Equanimity Hospital in Armageddon.

Twenty feet inside the hospital, we were stopped by what was likely a three hundred pound Sister of Equanimity who inquired as to our business. She was as handsome as a half-gallon bucket of toenail clippings.

Ruby didn't waste time with a preamble. She bosomed up to the Sister of Equanimity and said, "Where in the hell is Booger Red?"

Now, to pass the test and become a sister of Equanimity—I don't know—a person may well be required to walk around the world three times barefoot. I don't know. Whatever it takes likely wouldn't be easy. I have read my Bible some, so I know that some folks have had to do the best they could: in lions' dens, for goodness sakes, and fiery furnaces! I don't mean to put those saints down in any way, shape, nor form, but in my opinion, they got off easy. They were never required to stand bellybutton to bellybutton opposite Ruby.

The Sister eased off somewhat; maybe she received a divine premonition that Ruby could walk around the world three times barefoot carrying an ox on her back and doing handstands on the half hour. I don't know.

Ruby grasped this Equanimity's bead-infested crucifix tightly and explained that she, Ruby, understood and respected the Sister's love and devotion to the Lord. She further explained that if the nun did not get the hell out of the way, she stood a remarkably good chance of enjoying her Lord in eternal bliss before the sun went down.

Ruby even further explained, because she seemed to have gotten into an explaining frame of mind, the exact location where Sister might ultimately find her crucifix if she didn't move her fat butt in the direction of Booger Red.

Booger Red's face was as white as the bed sheet he was tucked into. Maybe only his bright red hair kept him from being completely invisible. Somehow, that red hair on that white sheet seemed to be almost an insult. And to Sister Equanimity, I expect it was.

A crucifix hung above his bed, and at the foot of the bed, facing Booger Red, was a picture of Jesus pointing at his bleeding heart. There was no way Booger Red could escape those accusing eyes. Those eyes would likely make an angel squirm and writhe. What they would do to the kingpin whiskey dealer of the Little Balkans, I could only guess.

Ruby picked up Booger Red's hand as if it were the most tender baby. He managed a "Howdy, Ruby." His eyes acknowledged Mr. Strang and then settled on me. He grinned. "Hello, you little fart." All those crinkle lines around his eyes bunched together, so I knew he meant it. Given the choice of having Booger Red call me a fart and having the Queen of England call me Sir Wally Gant—well, that old Queen of England would still be outside on the back step whining like a bob-tailed Airedale to get in.

The Sister of Equanimity had stayed in the background, but not without effort. When she could stand it no longer, she stepped up and said, "You will have to leave now. Mr. Passeggiata needs to rest." I expected Ruby to whirl around and damage Sister's jaw, but she didn't. She looked, solemn, into Booger Red's eyes and said, "I'll take care of everything."

From the hospital we drove to Booger Red's place of business. Ruby pulled a double-barreled shotgun from the back of the truck, produced a key, and we went in. She seemed to know right where the light switch was, and I felt better with the lights on. Ruby laid that shotgun on the bar in plain sight, then opened the front door for business.

Mr. Strang and I started back to Epic, leaving Ruby to spend the night in the bar. You might think I was apprehensive, leaving Ruby there alone, but I wasn't. No, sir, seeing Ruby standing behind the bar with her hand on that shotgun—well, if anything needed apprehensing about, it was Armageddon.

Next morning our newspaper, *The Buffalo County Trans-Weekly Disciplinarian*, came out to tell what everybody already knew:

Local Businessman Fatally Shot
—Recovery in Doubt

Mr. Pearl LaVern Passeggiata was shot in the back yesterday at his place of business in Armageddon....

The writer, Mr. Purvis Seymore, ranted on and on and, I guess, at the time it passed for news. But everyone knew—absolutely everyone who read *The Buffalo County Trans-Weekly Disciplinarian* knew—that the real news would come when Booger Red came out of the hospital and chewed off Purvis Seymore's nose for spreading the word that Booger Red was, in fact, Pearl LaVern Passeggiata.

12

Summer was passing faster than I wanted. I wasn't seeing much of Purdy Grundy, and I wasn't getting many steamboat nails straightened either. I felt guilty as sin about that, because I knew that down south there was a slave, biding his time breaking cane and depending on me. Dependence is a heavy load to lay on a boy.

My lessons on the silver B-flat cornet were discouraging, because there is a lot more to playing a silver B-flat cornet than I had previously anticipated. Miss Brownlow seemed enhanced with the idea of "ambrosia." Ambrosia is the right and proper way to blow spit through the rear end of a horn, and it don't come easy. She suggested that, both at home and at my lessons, I remove the mouthpiece from the horn and learn to spit ambrosia in an acceptable manner. She said it would save wear and stress on my silver B-flat cornet, and she was likely right. Still and all, I did not relish marching down Main Street on the Fourth of July spitting ambrosia through my mouthpiece without the aid and benevolence of my horn.

And that wasn't the worst of it. If you ever look closely at a sheet of music, you will see that, contrary to the way it sounds, music is mostly dots and squiggles, some with flags on the ends and some without. There are dots with even *two* flags on them, and some with no flags at all but a hole in the middle, for cripes sake! And numbers! Numbers and squiggles of every shape and discription. If there was anything in the world that Miss Brownlow seemed partial to, it was those squiggles. I had never thought of squiggles and numbers as what you might consider an integral part of music. She did. And she also told me that my valves were getting sticky, and I should have my dad buy some valve oil. In all truth and honesty, it appeared to me that Miss Brownlow was getting a little sticky herself.

Not only did she complain about my sticky valves, she complained that I did not spend enough time practicing. Now see, practicing was not that easy at our house. If I practiced inside, my dad would say, "Take that damn thing outside." When I practiced outside, our next-door neighbor would say, "Take that damn thing inside."

By the time I had finished with my third music lesson, my mom and dad had their enthusiasm in regard to my horn playing pretty much under control. My dad talked, more and more, about how if this family needed one more penny, he would have to take on a part-time job with the W.P.A. So I wasn't about to burden him with the expense of valve oil. I dabbed some 30 weight motor oil on each valve. It seemed like a good idea at the time, but it took all my finger strength to push them down, and an act of God would not have sprung them back up.

I washed each valve with coal oil until the motor oil was gone, and then I took a file and worked them over good. It wasn't long before those old valves were going up and down like a sewing machine, so I filed some more off. If you are smart and have a mechanical mind you can get by in this old world.

It is never a good thing to be a show-off, so I tried to look humble when I showed Miss Brownlow how well I had got my valves working. She tried them herself, and when they clanged a little from side to side, she went sort of pale. She didn't scream at me, and I was glad of that because I figured any scream coming out of *her* would be made up of dots and squiggles and maybe worse. But she likely had been practicing her ambrosia; she could sure spit her words out. "You are the most stupid boy I have ever seen. You have completely ruined your cornet!" To tell you the truth, she said several other things, but that was the nicest.

Well, she didn't appear to be in the mood to give me a lesson that day, so I packed up my silver B-flat cornet and went out the door. She stood in the doorway behind me, and I expected her to call out, "Goodbye." But she didn't; she hollered, "Don't come back!"

So I didn't tell *her* goodbye either.

13

After Booger Red was shot and Ruby assumed all the responsibilities in his business, Mr. Strang and I spent a lot of time on the road between Epic and Armageddon. We usually stopped at Galenaville, and, usually, Mr. Strang would turn off the main road, going east or west, to any one of a half dozen Little Balkan crossroad places like Cedar Rump or I'llbedamned or Betcherass. It didn't much matter, we could sell Ruby's Moon Butter any-where. See, we could stop our truck on the south edge of Dinglebutt, Kansas, and in three minutes a line would form. A lot of folks would even come over from North Dinglebutt, a full fifty feet back north. Life went on.

The next time I saw Booger Red, he looked a lot better. It's the Gospel truth that he wasn't Christmas-tree beautiful, but he looked better. The fat Sister of Equanimity was there, too, but she had changed. For one thing, she was more friendly to us. For another thing, she couldn't seem to keep her eyes off Booger Red. The crucifix still hung at the head of the bed, but the pic-ture of Jesus pointing at his bleeding heart was gone. In its place hung a remarkable pencil drawing of Booger Red pointing at his gold front tooth. Sister had done it herself, and it was a perfect likeness. Not quite hidden under the bed sheet, I could see the grip of what appeared to be a Colt .45 automatic pistol. Booger Red had been blind-sided once, but he was not likely to be blind-sided twice.

While big old Sister Equanimity fussed and refussed over Booger Red's pillow, Ruby caught his eye and patted her purse. Mr. Strang caught Booger's eye and patted a small bulge behind his belt. If Sister realized that three of the five people in the room were armed and should be considered dangerous, she didn't show the least sign of it.

Finally, Booger Red suggested to Equanimity that she should ease up on the pillows before they started bleeding. He said what he would like, more than anything in the world, would be a good glass of ice water. Sister did a genuflect and marched out of the room like she was going to slay a dragon. I figured her mind was trying to remember where she might have left her snow boots and her dog-sled, because, if there was no ice in the hospital, she would damn sure be on her way to Alaska.

Booger Red rolled his eyes upward and said, "Jesus H. Christ."

Ruby gave him a grin and said, "Better not say that in front of that nurse, or she's liable to go out and fetch him back!" I wanted to ask what the "H" stood for, but didn't dare. I knew enough to keep my mouth shut. I didn't fart either.

Ruby and Booger Red got their heads close and got right down to talking business. They laughed some and cussed some. About the only words I really picked up on were "Chicago Hot Shots." Mr. Strang stood back, picking his teeth like he didn't have a care in the world.

Sam Pulliam, the fellow who had shot my dad's goat, came in quiet as a low-drifting cloud. I missed his not so grand entrance, but Booger Red did not. First I knew was when, all of a sudden, Booger Red had that .45 in his hand pointed right at Mr. Pulliam's belly.

Booger Red used a few ear-wilting words and explained to Sam that unless he wanted a vent hole in his stomach, he had better make some noise when he came in.

Sam Pulliam was there on business, and it was pretty clear that kids were not included in *his* business. He glared at me like he had found a cooked worm on his ear of sweet corn.

Booger Red saw the look and said, "This here's Wally. He's my buddy and he's all right. Show Sam how you can fart, Wally."

Judas Priest! No doubt in my mind I turned red from top to bottom. But Booger Red motioned me to the bed and patted my back. "Wally works for Ruby, Sam, and so he works for me, too.

Mr. Sam Pullium was not the kind to smile much, and his eyes were blinking ninety miles an hour like as if he would just as soon erase me. But as I mentioned earlier, he was a stickler for having things done right. He stepped up and, as if he hadn't seen me a thousand times before, offered me his hand. "I'm pleased to meet you, Wally."

I told him, "Likewise, I'm sure," which my mom had drilled into me forever and ever, amen. Then, as far as Mr. Sam Pullium was concerned, I could have been a thistle in a cornfield nine miles west of town.

It worked out like this: Sam would be there to help Ruby run Booger Red's business. I wouldn't say that Ruby had exactly become a shadow of her former self from all the stress and strain, but she did look "tired."

Well, "tired" wasn't the only reason Ruby needed time off. And "tired" wasn't the reason Booger Red had called this meeting. The whole fact of the matter was that Buffalo County was on the brink of having a severe drought—of Moon Butter.

See, selling milk and Deep Shaft moonshine was a piddledy part of the Strang Dairy operation. It took me a while to realize that. I had slowly learned that Buffalo County and the whole rest of the Little Balkans seemed to revolve around moonshine; but remember Ruby was the only one on God's green earth who had the secret of making Moon Butter.

14

When Mr. Strang dropped me off at our back door, the first thing I saw was my dad looking defeated. His tool box was beside him, and he was abusing the kitchen screen door both by word and deed. My mom, at long last, had won the battle concerning screen door repair. She was all smiles. She was two-fingers-and-thumbing around a piecrust making ridges and valleys. "Wally! How was the milk route?"

"It went good," I told her.

"No," she said, "It went *well.*" See, this is one of the things I have never understood about mothers. If she already knew, then why did she ask? She was plainly in the mood to hear all there was to hear about the milk route business, so I had to think quick. You can rest assured that I was not about to relate my afternoon in the hospital with Booger Red, Sam Pullium, Ruby, and a truckload of deadly weapons. Sometimes you can just feel these things, and I knew this was not the time for me to explain how Sam Pullium nearly got a new vent in his stomach perpetrated by a .45 automatic. And, in as much as I had never heard her express a burning desire to learn about Chicago Hot Shots, I passed over that, too.

But I knew what she really wanted to hear, so I pulled on a long face and said, "I found another dead mouse in Mrs. Porter's icebox."

"Oh, my soul and body," she told me.

"And there were two cockroaches crawling across Mrs. Kenskey's kitchen table."

"Oh, Lord, NO!"

See, Mrs. Kenskey was Mom's best friend. Mom had eaten tuna sandwiches and Jell-O off the top of that table every third Thursday of the month. Well, I went on inventing about a shoebox full of mice and cockroaches and spreading them in a liberal fashion throughout every kitchen in Epic, until I figured I had better save some for my mom's enjoyment tomorrow.

Dad had the screen door off for the third or fourth time and was whittling at the bottom and the side again. "Tell her about the rats in the funeral home," he hollered to me.

But it appeared that my mom had heard adequate concerning the wild life of Epic, Kansas, so I said, "They were just little, tiny ones."

My dad had screwed the hinges back on the screen door and was ready for another test. He had stopped shouting at it, and that was a dangerous sign. He stood close to it and seemed to be in a quiet and earnest discussion. When that door dragged and hung up on a corner that had never appeared belligerent before, he simply said, "All right. All right. It's your decision!" Then, in three tries, he ripped it from its hinges and carried it to the driveway. The old Ford started the first time, and my dad drove it forward and backward over the screen door until you would have had to use a whisk broom and a dustpan to gather up enough of it for a Christian burial.

I went to bed proud and happy that night. Proud that I had been anointed into the Booger Red bootleg business. Happy because, at least in her mind, my mom had the only sanitary and pest-free house in Epic. Proud of my dad because he had proved that he was not one to take any guff from a screen door.

15

Next morning I rode my bicycle over to visit with Mose and Mew Washington, and on the way I met Miss Brownlow, my ex-silver-B-flat cornet-teacher. Out of politeness, I stopped to pass the time of day, but she just shook her head at me and admitted I was the absolute dumbest boy she had ever known.

"Well," I told her, "I may not be smart now, but I will grow into it." I clinched the argument by telling her, "My dad is smarter than a screen door!"

I guess she knew I had got the best of her because she made no reply whatsoever. She raised her nose in the air like you do when you think you maybe smell popcorn and marched on down the street. I raised my nose in the air also but could not detect the slightest fragrance of popcorn, so I pushed hard on the right pedal of my bicycle and sped off.

Mose sat there in his rocker, like always. But this time he had his leg propped up on a box; his face looked like the fuzzy last end of the dandelion season. That leg was poulticed and bright-feather-bedecked. A bowl of God-only-knows smoldered under it, sending brown smoke curling up. It was Mew's voodoo medicine, plain and simple.

"My toes is crampin' me up bad, Wally. Sometimes I almost wish I had my other leg back." See, it wasn't his real leg that was propped up and bright-feather-bedecked, it was his peg-leg. It was what Mose called his piss-elm leg. "I think it's this damn knot hole," he said, "I reckon its got a abscess in it."

Mew pulled me to one side and said, "Wally, you still workin' for Miz Ruby?"

"Yes, ma'am," I told her.

She pointed at the jug by Mose's rocker. "He's plumb out of his medicine, and that's the only thing will make him feel better. We don't gots no money."

"I'll be right back," I told her.

I headed for the dairy, and I just guess that old bicycle never moved so fast. I started hollering as soon as I turned up the driveway. "Ruby," I hollered, "Mose Washington's knot hole has got an abscess, and he's suffering pitiful. Can I take him a bottle and you take it out of my wages?"

Ruby almost grinned. "Is that the Mose Washington who gave you the steam whistle?"

"Yeah, and he's hurting bad."

Ruby brought out a quart of moonshine and also a half pint of Moon Butter. "You take this to old Mose. Tell him Ruby says to take care of his knot hole. It won't come out of your wages, either."

That's the way Ruby is. Given the need, like, maybe in Armageddon, she would shotgun the back end off a Chicago Hot Shot, but if a good fellow needed a little medicine for a sore knot hole, Ruby was first in line to offer solace and recompense.

I handed the bottle and the Moon Butter to Mew, and she laid her hand soft on my head. "You're a good friend, Wally," she told me.

"Miss Brownlow says I'm the dumbest boy she ever saw," I said.

"Well," Mew said, "I don't know no Miss Brownlow, but I expect she be a white lady."

Mew poured a cheese glass full for Mose, and he drank it down like a trooper. I do honestly believe I could see that old wooden leg stop throbbing.

Mose gave me a grin, and when he talked, his breath could have loosened bricks on a silo. "Ain't nothin' better for cramped toes and a abscessed knot hole," he told me. He held his glass out to Mew and said, "Woman, a bird can't fly on one wing!"

I left the front porch when Mose started snoring. Mew stepped inside, and when she came back, she handed me a bright green feather. "Hang this over your bed, Wally." She didn't tell me why, and I didn't ask, but I hung that feather over my bed, and as near as I could tell, it worked exactly like it was supposed to.

16

Now, I will tell you this, had Eli Whitney had helpers like Purdy Grundy, he would not have got the steamboat invented in thirty-six thousand years.

The closer it came to the end of summer vacation, the less enthusiasm Purdy seemed to have for straightening steamboat nails. In point of fact, as you might say, steamboats, slaves, rivers, and most other worthwhile causes had sort of slid from Purdy's predilection.

Purdy, on the best of days, with a hammer in his hand, was a red-flag, bridge-out, cyclone-coming danger zone. But we sat there, one afternoon, straightening nails, and Purdy was hitting his finger about as often as he was hitting the nail. I know it was unkind of me, but if you've only got a few weeks left to build a steamboat, find a dingle-brained river, and preserve a slave from the clutches of a canebrake—it just doesn't leave much time for Christian forbearance.

"Purdy," I finally said, "are you trying to straighten nails or are you trying to straighten your fingers?" Well, it was very unlike Purdy to ignore such an unseemly misdemeanor, but his mind was far and away. "Wally," he said, "If you ever tell anybody this I will kill you, but...have you ever heard of being in love?"

"I have," I told him. But I was honest enough to admit I didn't know much about it. "Does it make a fellow want to hit his fingers with a hammer?" I had to ask because that seemed to be his predominate affliction.

"Sometimes maybe it does." he said. "At first I thought I had caught Infantile Psoriasis, but my legs haven't withered, so I guess I'm in love."

"Goddamn!" I admonished, and I'm sorry I said that because I have never been one to take the Lord's name in vain unless it was absolutely necessary. It never crossed my mind to tease or poke fun at poor old Purdy. It was plain to see that he had troubles enough. I will confess that I scooted a few inches further away from him because for all I knew, love might be contagious. I was smart enough to know that contagious is a terrible thing to catch.

Maybe all this is what "growing up," means, I thought. I had seen Booger Red lying near shot to death in a white Equanimity bed. I had been present when two G-men chose death by a W.P.A. bridge in preference to Ruby's "Blue Yodel." And now I was being forced to watch my best friend in the throes of love.

"Who?" I finally asked.

Purdy gulped and said, "I'll kill you if you ever tell— Loris Admuson."

"Goddamn!" See, I said it for the second time in the same day and said it with no qualms or regrets. I figured that if God knew Loris Admuson, he would understand and agree. Loris Admuson's hair was long and so white it was spooky. The rest of her, such as was available for viewing, was as white as the underbelly of a frog. Her eyes were like transparent marbles.

"Purdy," I said. "You can't be in love with Loris Admuson; she's an albingo!"

Purdy sat and considered my reasonableness. Finally he said, "If I can't be in love with her because she's an albingo, then why do I keep hitting my fingers with a hammer?"

Well, he flat-out had me there.

Purdy headed for home with his head down, doubtless pondering if his life was ruined forever. I straightened a few more nails, but I couldn't seem to get Loris Admuson out of my mind. The fact of the matter was, she *was* pretty. She was a lot more fun to be around than any other girl I knew. In all fairness, I reminded myself, if Loris happens to be of the albingo persuasion, it's likely not her fault.

It came as a great relief when my mom called me to supper; I had hammered my finger three times while thinking about Loris.

17

Next morning, before my scrambled eggs and Vienna sausages had found a comfortable resting place in my stomach and got prepared for their next adventure, Mr. Strang and I headed south toward Armageddon. We were about a mile south of Cedar Rump and three miles north of I'llbedamned when the left rear tire went flat and set up a terrible commotion.

Mr. Strang was not, at best, what you might deem to be a jovial man. And on that morning, if he weren't suffering the pangs of a purple carbuncle, a canker sore, and an in-grown toenail, I would be very much surprised.

I dragged out the jack and the jack-handle. Mr. Strang dragged out the spare tire, which he slammed down so hard it bounced over into the ditch. That was all it took.

Mr. Strang snatched the jack-handle from my hand and waved it at the sky. "All right!" he shouted. He shouted loud, and I understood why. God has a lot of ground to cover; He might be off answering prayers in Albuquerque or in Nova Scotia. Wherever he was, it is my undying belief that he could hear Mr. Strang without straining his ears.

"I don't want any more trouble today," he shouted. "I don't want it and I won't tolerate it. If I have any more trouble today, Ruby will come up there and stomp your damn Pearly Gates into matchsticks. She will bust your stone tablets to smithereens and pluck the pin-feathers off your angels!"

I guess I stood there with my mouth wide open. In my Methodist mind I had no doubt that six thousand lightning bolts would come down, and Wally Eugene Gant would be naught but a lovely memory.

But it didn't happen. I doubt Mr. Strang was very worried; he was more used to dealing with Ruby than with God. Ruby was the "here and now." God was only a "maybe."

Don't get me wrong I'm not knocking the benefits of divine supplication in any way, shape, or form, but I will tell you this: Mr. Strang was explaining, not supplicating. And in all the time I've been with the Strang Dairy, we've never had another flat tire.

We went on south, making our usual stops at Betcherass and Disaster City. At Mulespit, Tall DeCastro's place was shut up tight because Tall had been shot and killed the night before. It was a blow to the Strang dairy, because Tall sold a lot of Moon Butter, and he still owed us for some of it. Mr. Strang said Tall had better be completely and irrevocably dead or Ruby would likely come down and break his arm. He figured she might anyway.

First off in Armageddon, we stopped at the Sisters of Equanimity Hospital. Booger Red had just taken his first steps since his "Fatally Shot—Recovery in Doubt," experience. I knew he was in pain because his face was as white as Loris Admuson's. Well, sir, as soon as I thought that, I was sorry for the thought. My finger was still sore from the Loris Admuson hammering I had given it last night.

Sister of Equanimity gave us a welcoming smile. She knew we were friends of Booger Red and had grown used to our almost daily vicissitudes.

Booger Red told us we could talk in front of Sister because he had explained the whole situation. She knew that the Chicago Hot Shots were out to kill him and take over his business. In her bosom there was now an extra bulge; it looked very much like a small revolver.

"It's awful bad times," Booger Red told us. "Strangers all over the place; they're after everything I got, and not a damn thing I can do about it." We told him about Tall DeCastro getting killed, but he already knew. I blurted out that Mr. DeCastro's troubles weren't necessarily over yet because he owed us Moon Butter money and Ruby might still come down and break his arm. For the first time that day Booger Red smiled. "Wally," he said, "I just expect she might."

Mr. Strang inquired as to whether there had been any trouble in Booger Red's own personal establishment, and Booger Red grinned again. "No, sir," he said, "Sam Pullium went to Fort Scott and hired us a mean-looking little hunchback midget. He sets him on top of the bar with a shotgun, and it's so quiet in there you could hear an angel pissing off the edge of a cloud."

Sister tittered and blushed. "Red, angels don't do that!"

"Well, of course they do!" he indignated. "They just step behind a big old thunderhead, unbutton their feathers and..."

But sister was gone. We left soon after also. Booger Red lay there shouting for Sister to come back. "Damn it," he shouted, "Even an angel can't hold it forever! Sister, get back in here!"

On the way to the truck I weighed Sister's understanding of hundreds of years of Church wisdom against Booger Red's practical knowledge of how things worked. It was too deep for me; but by and large, I tended to go along with Booger Red. I was careful not to walk under any clouds, and I couldn't help wondering if our windshield wiper worked.

18

I scarce ever climbed to the top of the barn to sing any-more. Miss Maudie and Edmond Denny, through their own deviation of duty, had not driven down the right road at the right time. WIBW was doomed to be reft of me. I was sorry for them, but it was not my fault.

My wages from the Strang Dairy had been raised to a dollar-fifty a week, and even my mom was proud. In all honesty, it wasn't so much *me* she was proud of. She was proud of herself for having the insight to know that *milk* was the pathway to success and glory. If you had asked my mom what the Holy Trinity consisted of, I expect she would have said, "The Father, the Son, and—Milk."

Of course, there was no way on this green earth I could ever have told her the reason for my escalated value at the dairy. Not in a million years could I tell her I was a valued spoke in the wheel of bootleggery and was becoming friends with a Catholic Sister. See, every boy is born with an inkling of what a mom should be told and what a mom should not. My inborn inkling told me that, by and large, moms did not want to hear about a

Sister of Equanimity who nourished a revolver to her bosom; did not need to know that Tall DeCastro lay stiff and cold with a ninety percent chance of still having his arm broken.

No, I told her about finding a mole which had tunneled into Mrs. Karswain's refrigerator and was eating her cabbage hand-over-fist. I told her how I grabbed that mole by the tail and flung it over into Mr. Brown's back yard. Mr. Brown was not a subscriber to the Strang Dairy delivery route and so it served him right. I created a cockroach here, a dead mouse there. In a burst of generosity, I allowed a rotting cantaloupe in the preacher's kitchen, until my mom finally screeched, "Wally, stop!"

With the pretty sure feeling that my presence was no longer required, I kicked the bottom of where the screen door used to be before my dad fixed it. We all did that—we kicked the used-to-be screen door. Even my mom would still kick the lower part of the air and say, "I just hate this screen door."

My dad was in the living room fiddling with the radio. Earlier he had broken the tuning-knob off, and the last thing I heard as I went outside, he was shouting, "Where the hell is the Lone Ranger?"

After supper I pumped up my bicycle tire and headed toward Loris Admuson's. I had restrained my abomination concerning slavery and my growing abomination of nail straightening and, therefore, I had not hammered my fingers lately because of thinking about Loris Admuson. Ending slavery was turning out to be more of a problem than I had anticipated, and I could only hope that those poor cane-breakers had developed the Christian virtue of patience.

I circled the block two times before I saw her. When I did see her, she was standing amidst a patch of hollyhocks by her dad's potato patch. Watching me! She stood out like a vanilla wafer in a plate full Oreos.

I stood with all my weight on the right pedal of my bicycle, going in circles and spreading gravel. I sped like a P-38 Lockheed Lightning, because that's what I was. If there was one Jap fighter pilot in fifty-two who could have shot me down, I would have been very much surprised.

I coasted up to her as slow and gentle as I could. You have to be careful, because the least little thing will spook an albingo. It crossed my mind to wonder why in the world I was there anyway. I concluded that, like it or not, I was just plain and simple magnetically preordinated toward albingos. But, see, what in the world do you say to a hollyhock-patch-standing albingo who is also a girl?

I was spared the expedition of finding the first words. She gave me a smile. What you might call a *tentative* smile, but still, a smile. Then she spoiled the whole thing by saying, "Wally, what is six times six?" Now, see, just leave it to a dingle-brained albingo woman to go for your soft white underbelly!

I felt my face go red. Somewhere in my mind I knew what six times six was. It was there. Somewhere. Six times six? Everybody on God's green earth knows what equals six times six. I had not spent the better part of my life in school, day in and day out, learning what six times six was, just to have it gone. Or else what was education for? See, get asked by a Baptist or a Presbyterian what is six times six and the answer rolls off your tongue. Give me a clear day, with no wind, and precious few people if any can stump me, six-times-six-wise. But get asked six times six by a girl albingo who is standing near a potato patch, and it fuzzies up your mind. Why hadn't she had the common decency to ask me what seven times seven was? I could do that one blindfolded. "How many biscuits can you eat? Forty-nine and a ham of meat."

I plucked up the first grasshopper that came to hand and flicked it at her. She screamed, as all albingos do when confronted with a grasshopper. I plucked and flicked another. She ran toward her back porch, and I didn't care because I had about had it with six-times-six albingos.

Plucking and flicking grasshoppers at albingos is punishable by seventeen years in prison, and if they are wearing glasses, it's even worse. But I didn't care.

It is a tribute to my eternal regret that I did not think to challenge her back with "What is eleven times eleven?" That would have settled her hash, because nobody in the whole world knows the answer to that!

Albingos are a lot like goats, only lacking their pleasant personality.

19

It was near ten in the morning when Mr. Strang and I pulled into Betcherass. There was a crowd of people gathered around Minor Angel Allegucci's roll-brick-covered Pool and Snookertorium. Minor Angel had just got the tip of his nose shot off by a Chicago Hot Shot, and if there is anything in the world that would draw a bigger crowd than that I would be hard pressed to explain what it might be.

Mr. Allegucci made some of the best Deep Shaft in Buffalo County, and the assault on his business and his nose was an affront to all.

What had happened was this: Three strangers came in and ordered drinks of whiskey. Then they ordered meatballs, and Mr. Allegucci told them the meatballs weren't ready yet. And the fat one, the grouchy one, said, "What kind of a rinky-dink place is this that the meatballs aren't ready?" He spread five twenty-dollar bills on the table and laid a revolver on top of them. "We just bought your business," he said. "You'd best start looking for a job."

Mr. Minor Angel Allegucci excused himself and said he would go check on those meatballs. He was back in no time at all, carrying a whole big kettle of steaming meatballs, which he distributed without partiality on their Chicago heads. That was when he got the tip of his nose shot off.

An eye witness told that the culprits had escaped death-by-meatball in a black Chevrolet, and so folks spread out and looked for one of those. Even in Betcherass a black Chevrolet was not hard to find. The first one discovered belonged to old man Ralph Skinks, who could quote the Bible forward and backhand.

The citizens of Betcherass surrounded Mr. Skinks' car and, as was right and proper, broke out the right front headlight because enough is enough. Mr. Skinks, old as he was, climbed up on the hood and announced, "Four score and seven years ago!" Not a soul in the crowd could argue against that. So he proceeded to reassure any who might have been wondering that Adam had begat Seth and lived nine hundred and thirty years. There was some applause, but not as much as you might expect. And then, as if that news weren't enough to raise blisters, Mr. Skinks bedazzled everyone that good old Seth had, on his own recognizance, begat Enos and still lived nine hundred and twelve years. Then Mr. Skinks climbed down, found half a brick, and broke out the left headlight on his own Chevrolet.

I couldn't help but grin and feel secure. I figured it would just be quite a while before anymore Chicago tough guys dared try to take over the Betcherass Pool and Snookertorium.

Mr. Allegucci told Mr. Strang and me that he had never before in his life got five twenty-dollar bills for one kettle of meatballs. He said if his nose just held out he would be able to retire by the first of the year.

We unloaded a big order of Moon Butter and headed south, toward Armageddon.

20

Next morning, Pard Adams from the lumberyard brought over a new screen door to replace the one my dad had irrevocably repaired. My mom pointed him to the driveway—to the bones and gristle remnants of the old screen door. Mr. Pard Adams smiled in admiration.

"You are a fortunate woman to be married to a man as smart as Wilson Gant," he told her. "I guess you would just not believe how many men are of the opinion that they can fix a screen door. But they can't! God has created more wonders than are countable, but He has never yet created a man who can repair a screen door."

My mom, who had been on the verge of explaining her own personal views of screen door reparations, was mollified. She appeared proud in a sort of humble way.

Mr. Adams, who was a Deacon in the church, explained that screen doors were, as part of their inborn nature, "recalcitrant." He exemplified that the word "recalcitrant" had, mainly and for the most part, been invented because of the screen doors encountered in the Book of Revelation. He said those holy screen doors had been about as recalcitrant as any screen doors you might ever hope to find.

"No, sir," he said, "The only proper way you can deal with a broke screen door is to run over it fifty or sixty times with a T model Ford."

The new screen door swung free and easy. My mom was happy. She had the radio turned up loud and was singing along with Vernon Dalhart, explaining what she would do if she had the wings of an angel. The big skillet was on the stove waiting for the weenies. The little skillet was waiting to reheat the cottage cheese.

But when my dad got home from work he had forgotten to buy the weenies, and my mom told him that he was a pure and simple recalkatrant.

"Now, just what the hell is that supposed to mean?" he asked. He asked because, if he was at all guilty of the sin of pride, it was the pride of knowing words.

"Well," she told him, "If you men would just spend more time reading the Book of Revolution, you would know that 'recalkatrant' is a fellow who forgets to buy the weenies!"

Later my dad came out with me and straightened a few nails. He hammered his fingers a few times also, but I don't believe his mind was on Loris Admuson.

21

I hadn't been home from the milk route more than twenty minutes when Purdy Grundy rode up on his bicycle, all cocklebur-bristled. He struck a pose like John L. Sullivan waiting to be photographed and socked me square in the eye.

I didn't even try to hit him back because I was admiring all the stars and rainbows I was seeing. When it appeared that there was still some chance I might live, I said, "Now, why in the world did you do that?"

"I did that," he told me, "because you flicked grasshoppers at Loris Admuson."

I don't like to brag, but I was man enough to admit that I had.

I struck a pose, maybe somewhat less impressive than that of the late, lamented John L. Sullivan, but, still, nothing to be ashamed of if a fellow has just been struck in the eye. Then I set out to explain the facts of life to stupid, ex-friend Purdy Grundy.

"Well," I inquired, "What in the damn-blasted-hell would you do if you rode up with the best of intentions,

and an albingo person was standing between the hollyhocks and the potato patch, and, without provocation,
asked you what was six times six?"

Purdy blinked, plainly in disbelief that his dearly
beloved would propose such a personal indiscretion. I
will tell you this: if there had been a handful of
grasshoppers ready at hand, I would have flicked them
all at old Purdy Grundy and never looked back.

As it was, Purdy still seemed to have some fight left in
him. It is hard to let go of a dream. So I kicked him in
the ankle as hard as I could. I took advantage of his dis-
equilibrium and rubbed his nose in what was left of the
screen door. In all honesty and modesty, I will tell you
that if anyone could grind and prepare a screen door for
nose-rubbing better than my dad, I would be very much
surprised.

Next day, Mr. Strang looked at my black eye and said,
"Judas Priest, what in the world happened to you?"

All my life I have been trained in the use of honesty, so
I told him flat out: "Purdy Grundy slugged me because I
flang grasshoppers at his albingo girlfriend." At first I
thought he had started a grin, but he soon sobered.

"Judas Priest," he told himself, and me, somewhat.
"As if I don't have enough trouble, I have hired a felon!
Are you sure it was an albingo?"

"Well," I said. "She is whiter than anything you ever
saw, and she has pink, glassy eyes that don't seem to
have a behind to them."

"Oh, Lord," he said, "now, let me get this straight. You
flang grasshoppers at an albingo right here in Buffalo
County?"

I told him that that was about the size of it.

"Wally," he said, and he was dead serious, "of all the
places in the whole world you could have chosen to fling
grasshoppers at an albingo, you had to chose Buffalo

County? Judas Priest! The good people of Buffalo County just won't tolerate that crap! Why, in 1903 they *hanged* a fellow down in Armageddon for flinging grasshoppers at an albingo!" He watched me out of the corner of his eye. I guess he wanted to make sure I didn't jump out of the moving truck and make a dash for the border. Then he said, "Ok, Ruby is good friends with the judge. Maybe he can order a change of venue."

I felt my ears go red because there are some things too personal to talk about. "Well," I told him, "I just guess we won't need to bother the judge. My mom makes me change my "venues" every morning because she says if I get hit by a truck, I will be a disgrace to the whole family and she won't be able to show her face in town."

Not more than three miles down the highway, parked beneath an old dead cedar tree, sat Sheriff Tom Guffey. He was waiting for us and there was no doubt in my mind that I was about to pay the horrible price for cruelty to albingos.

From the look on Sheriff Guffey's face I knew it was going to be bad, but he didn't even look at me. He looked hard at Mr. Strang. "Don't go down south, Jesse," he warned. "Sam Pullium has been found floating face down in a mine pit, and Booger's Emporium is shot full of holes from hell to breakfast. Them Chicago boys is taking over."

I guess you could have kicked Mr. Strang in the stomach and he wouldn't have looked any worse.

"Sam Pullium," he said, almost too quiet to hear, "That's the sorriest news I ever heard—and the Emporium! I'm obliged to you for letting me know, Tom. And Ruby is obliged too."

Mr. Strang reached over his shoulder and pulled out a pint of Moon Butter. The Sheriff took it without the flicker of the eye and grinned, "Hell fire, Jesse, I'd do the same for a white man."

Mr. Strang turned the truck around and headed back toward Epic. I could tell he was sad. So was I. He drove slowly. I guess if you're not going anywhere, there's no need to hurry.

22

He drove right past my house without letting me out. Maybe he had forgotten I was sitting there right beside him. I would have as soon smashed my thumb as be there when Ruby heard all the bad news we were bringing. But I wasn't in any mood to go home and invent a bunch of cockroaches and dead mice to please my mom, either.

We rolled up that rough-rutted old driveway, stopped, and just sat there. Mr. Strang pulled the key from the ignition and stared at it. He fingered it and rubbed it as if it were Aladdin's lamp—and looked like he wished to God he could have three wishes. I knew what the first one would be.

Ruby was in her secret room, making Moon Butter, so we had to holler her out. Nobody on God's green earth was allowed into the Moon Butter room. I had no idea how she would react to all this new trouble, but I was braced to run.

She didn't look happy to be interrupted, but with one look at Mr. Strang and me, she seemed to know that she was going to be more unhappy. Mr. Strang told her everything in mighty few words. Ruby just sucked a noisy breath from somewhere down deep. It wasn't good to hear. She sort of wilted herself down onto an old bench and stared out at far beyond nothing. Mr. Strang and I just stood like a couple of dead stumps by a creek bank and waited. You can bet I didn't take my eyes off her, so I saw Ruby change.

Her shoulders started to straighten and she seemed to be swelling up like somebody was using a tire pump on her. "All right!" she finally said. "All right!" But I knew she wasn't meaning everything was all right. What she was meaning was: *All right, you Chicago Hot Shots, you asked for it!*

Well, sir, I'd heard about someone's eyes flashing like lightning, but up until then I had never witnessed it. And while her eyes flashed like lightning, her face was clouding up like those dark-ugly clouds that come in from the southwest. The ones that make my mom check the storm cellar door to make sure it still works. The ones that may bring strong winds and hail. The ones that can kill.

"Wally," she said. She said it quiet. Scary quiet. "I'm going to be needing you more. Can you start coming over at eight every morning?"

I told her I wasn't sure because my mom always rousts me out about that time to tend the goats.

Ruby thought a minute. "Wally, are you fond of them goats?"

"I hate them," I admitted.

"Is your dad fond of them goats?" In all honesty I had to tell her that Dad didn't really like them either.

"Wally, is your mom fond of them goats?"

I told her that my mom was not quite so fond of them as I.

"Then, why in the *hell* does your family keep GOATS?"

"Well, my dad bought them to teach me responsibility."

On another day she might have more to say about goats and responsibility, but today she had other things on her mind. "Jesse, tomorrow I want you to see Wilson Gant and buy them goats. Tell him that working for Ruby will teach Wally more responsibility than all the goats in Buffalo County. Tell him that from now on Wally will be making three dollars a week.

"You go on home now, Wally, and remember to keep your mouth shut. Folks will be hearing things soon enough."

I walked back home feeling pretty downcast. Not downcast about the goats, but about all the killings and trouble. I knew my mom would take one look at me and know right off the bat that something was wrong. All the cockroaches and dead mice in the world wouldn't fool her today. What I needed was the most powerful idea I could think of, something that would knock her mind plum slanch-wise. It hit me just as I reached our yard. Multiplication tables! That good old Loris Admuson had flat saved my bacon.

My mom took one look and, just like I knew she would, said, "Wally, are you all right?"

"I'm fine, it's just that I've been thinking."

She leaned her dust mop against the wall and took a closer look at me. What she had just heard was enough to start tilting her mind slanch-wise.

"School will be starting pretty quick, and I figured it wouldn't hurt if I sort of looked over my multiplication tables."

"Wally," she almost shouted, "That's the most responsible thing I ever heard you say!" I don't guess Jesus Himself ever got a sweeter smile from His mother.

See, now, what I figure happened next was this: the word *responsible* had triggered something in her mind. "It's the milk!" she cried. "The wonderful, glorious healing power of milk has made you responsible! I'll go find your arithmetic book!" And she sailed off singing "He's been saved by the milk of the lamb." She plain didn't know much about the dairy business, but she couldn't have been happier if I'd been triplets.

23

When we went to bed that night clouds were rolling in, dark enough to inspire my mom to set out the coal oil lamp just in case. I pulled off my shoes and socks and rubbed the black stuff out from between my toes.

I will tell you that old bed felt pretty good. The window was open, and the breeze blowed in glorious. Summer-warm-wet is as good as a smell gets, all of the out-of-doors smelling like wet acorns.

All through the day I had done a good job keeping Sam Pullium out of my mind. I can't say we had ever been real friends. However, there in the dark, I couldn't seem to think about anything but him. See, I never before knew anyone who had actually died. Of course, I knew that people died, but not people I knew.

Well, now that I think about it, that's not quite true. I sort of remember when my Great Uncle Lewis died. My dad lifted me up so I could see down into the coffin. I will tell you this: there wasn't a great of a lot of difference, Uncle Lewis alive or Uncle Lewis dead.

Still and all, it changes things, dying does. Sheriff
Tom Guffey had said, "floating face down in a mine pit."
I could see him there, Sam Pullium. Not doing a breast-
stroke, not even a dog paddle. Just there, face down. No
wind and no waves in a mine pit, just face down in the
quiet dark. Old Sam Pullium! But I shouldn't call him
that any more. He was dead, he was *Mr.* Sam Pullium
now. Mr. Sam Dead Pullium.

And it weighed on me that I owed him a personal debt.
Him, having shot the dang peeing goat off the dang
hearse. Him, having saved me from slaving in what
amounted to the same as a canebrake, except, in my
case, he more likely he saved me from one third of a
"goatbrake."

Maybe our whole family owed him a debt. Anyone in
town could get a laugh from my dad just by mentioning
Mr. Pullium shooting that goat.

My mom, having declared that she would never again
be able to show her face in public, had adapted to a
remarkable extent. If anything, she was holding her
head up higher than normal. No, sir, I believe if any of
the women at her club, the "Golden Circle Quilting,
Recipe Exchange, and Christian Endeavourment Club,"
had mentioned that goat, my mom would have said,
"Well! I would rather have a dead goat, than cockroaches or dead mice in my refrigerator! Is there any
more Jell-O?"

But, dang it, how could Sam Pullium be dead? Dead
goes on for a long time.

The thought nagged. I owed him. Is a debt unpaid like
a bed unmade? Waiting?

Cold mine pit water splashed my face. From somewhere I heard the thunder of gun shots ripping through
Booger Red's Emporium. When the lightning came I
could see Mr. Sam Pullium at the foot of my bed, just

standing there, looking at me. Not looking mean or anything like that, understand, just looking—dead. Then it started to rain.

My mom came in and closed the window and said she hoped to goodness the curtains hadn't got blowed against that rusty screen because if they had they would be ruined and we couldn't afford any new curtains because we had already had to buy a new back screen door and why did all this have to happen to her?

I mean no offense to the memory of Sam Pullium, but it was a great relief when my mom turned on the light and somewhat shooed him from my bedroom. I went back to a wet-pillow sleep, but things didn't get much better. Purdy Grundy was soon hitting me in the eye and, in the background, I could hear Loris Admuson chanting, "Six times six is thirty-six. Six times six is thirty-six."

Just stop! See if you can think of three people on God's green earth—besides my teacher, and my Aunt Helen—who give a flying damn if six times six is thirty-six. Find even *two* people who would blink an eye if they read in the newspaper that six times six is one-hundred-and-twenty-seven million! Good luck! Go farther, go into the universe and ask anyone you meet between Alpo and Penumbra what is six times six. You will get a blank look. You think those Alpo and Penumbra people care? I would be very much surprised. Six times six is the dumbest thing I can think of. Still and yet, my dad maintains that mathematics is important! Not for the betterment of dreams, it's not!

Mr. Strang knocked on the back door as my dad was finishing his first cup of coffee. The rain had stopped, but my mom, who knew etiquette when she saw one, said, "My goodness, come in here before you get soaked.

And watch out you don't brush against that brand new screen door because it has fresh paint on it."

She set a cup of hot coffee in front of him and inquired if he took cream.

"Yes, Ma'am," he told her, "If you happen to have some."

"Oh, I have some all right. It's the best cream in the world. It comes from the Strang Dairy. My son, Wally, is an employee there." If my mom couldn't make a joke, I would be hard pressed to know who could. Mr. Strang managed a grin, but I think it hurt him.

He turned to my dad, Mr. Strang did, and said, "Wilson, I'd like to discuss your goats." I could see my dad clinch up. Not many days went by without some or another neighbor stopped by wanting to discuss my dad's goats. Not many days went by without one or both of those goats escaping their obligation and running hell bent and what you might call "amok." Amok is a terrible thing to run.

They went through flower beds and gardens, blithely and without prejudice: Protestants, Catholics, Methodists, and Baptists all suffered. Even the Holy Rollers, who had moved a small shed down by the low-water bridge until they could get their tabernacle built, did not complain about a scarcity of goats. My dad's goats bounded and abounded. What those goats didn't eat they trampled, and what they didn't trample they pissed on. In fairness, most usually, they did all three, without malice or forethought.

"See," Mr. Strang explained, "day after tomorrow is Ruby's birthday. We've got cows enough to last a lifetime, but Ruby doesn't give a whistle for cows. No, sir, Ruby has always wanted goats. What I was thinking is this: if you could see your way clear to sell me your goats, for Ruby's birthday, I would certainly be obliged."

Before my dad had a chance to tell Mr. Strang that there was no way on God's green earth that he could part with those goats, that they were like part of the family, Mr. Strang bemoaned. "Also," he bemoaned, "we're terrible busy at the dairy right now, and if Wally didn't have to take care of those goats, we could use him more hours and pay him three dollars a week."

My dad pulled a sad, poker face, and considered. Maybe I was the only one in the room who knew—but I was pretty sure. If my dad had just been given notice that the roll was about to be called up yonder and that he, my dad, was first in line to sit at the right hand of God, he could not have have been more pleased.

My dad rested his forehead in his cross-fingered hands and shook his head. "Anybody but Ruby," he said, "and I wouldn't do it. But Ruby is about the finest woman I know, so...I'll sell."

My mom's nose rose appreciably, and she asked if anybody wanted more hot coffee. My dad said he figured he could use maybe half a cup. And, likely because her glasses were out of date, she poured it mostly on his hand.

Then began the haggling and the dickering. My dad, realizing how much he hated those goats, held out, absolutely, for considerably less than he had paid for them. Mr. Strang offered more than any eleven goats in all the world were worth. My mom, maybe to seal the deal, asked again if anyone wanted more coffee. Mr. Strang said, "Just a tad more, please." My dad rubbed his reddened hand and said he reckoned he'd had enough.

We tied the goats behind the dairy truck and Mr. Strang drove slow, leading them, goat-bitching, all the way to the dairy. There's no way under the light of the living sun I could guarantee it, but I knew that back

home, my dad was jumping, clicking his heels, kissing
the dandelions, kissing the pump handle, kissing the
rose trellis—kissing the Model T Ford, which he would
have done anyway because he was partial to it.

My dad would have broke into song. He would be
dancing. He would be singing :
  "No more goats, no more goats,
  No more goats on Sunday,
  No more goats, no more goats,
  Gotta get your goats filled Monday.
  Or Tuesday, or Wednesday, or Thursday,
  Or, what the hell."
He would raise his hands to the sky and say, "Blessed
art thou, mother of God, and blessed be my Fruit of the
Looms."

And my mom would say, "Wilson! Wilson. I'm glad as
you are to be rid of those goats, but I wish you wouldn't
talk Catholic."

24

Mr. Strang drove slow with the tied-behind goats following along just as nice and innocent as if they were going to their first communion. One dainty hoof before another.

They were regular "Peace on Earth, Good Will to Men" goats. Mr. Strang kept his eye on them through the rear view mirror and grinned at their cuteness all the way home. I couldn't see them and I didn't want to. They couldn't see me, either, but I could feel their devil-goat evil eyes boring into my back. My best hope was that I would be there watching the first time one of those goats caught him with his back turned and butted him ass over appetite.

Mr. Strang, with what I knew to be misguided and unwarranted enthusiasm, had spread fresh straw all over the ground in the pen where the goats would be tied. He had laid gunny sacks under the barn roof overhang, making a cozy bed for them. The goats, being goats, showed their gratitude by peeing on the straw and then starting to eat the gunny sacks. Mr. Strang waved his hat and hollered "Hey, Now! Hey!"

I started toward the house, leaving them to get acquainted. A boy with a mean streak might have grinned.

Ruby met me at the door and showed no interest whatsoever in her birthday goats. She held out a Bible and asked me to put my hand on it and swear I would uphold and forever keep secret the secret secrets of the Strang Dairy. The Bible was in German, so I wasn't sure it really counted. However, Ruby told me that the Bible had belonged to her grandma and pointed to the date "1848." She said that if that Bible had been good enough for her grandma, it was good enough for her. She said that swearing on a German Bible was more serious than swearing on the English variety, and anyone who broke an oath taken on a German Bible would be crucified, null, and void.

Well, Ruby was my boss, so I put my hand on that Bible and said, "Sonofabitch." It was about the best I could do.

Still, Ruby seemed to be pondering. I guess she was not quite sure, either, of the power of the Holy Word if it happen to be sifted through the German. So, she placed my hand on one of the machine gun bullets that her brother, Howard, had absconded from Camp Leonard Wood in lieu of an honorable discharge—a sort of holy relic.

Ruby plainly wanted to do things right, so she demanded that I take my oath all over again, and include that I was neither a Jap nor a Nazi, and that I would wash my hands on a regular basis whether or not they seemed to need it.

"Yes, ma'am," I told her, "Sonofabitch!"

There are mighty few things can make a fellow feel as warm and sanctified as swearing an oath. I was willing and able to build on and expand mine, but Ruby seemed satisfied and turned away to lay the Bible on the table. Therefore, she didn't hear me when I double sealed my promise by whispering, "Piss and fart."

Ruby looked at me sad. "Wally, I'm sorry to get you mixed up in all this. I thought all the shootings and killings had ended years ago, but they're back."

She fished down into what you might call her "cleavage" and found a key, which unlocked the biggest padlock I have ever seen. It was on the heavy door of the Moon Butter room! Not President Roosevelt, not Knute Rockne, not even Red Skelton would have ever been allowed inside the Moon Butter room. But *I* was there. *Me*: Wally Eugene Gant.

I knew, somewhat, but only somewhat, about Moon Butter. I had taken my oath on a German Bible to keep my mouth shut and neither wild horses, sleet, nor dark of night could have made me reveal anything I saw. But what I saw was mostly a pile of pots and pans that needed to be scrubbed and polished nearly to the point of extinction.

Were it not that I didn't want to use all my oath words on the first day of my new job, I would have sworn that I also saw a fence post with a black beard fade back into the shadows.

25

I guess Epic is not much different from any small town. There are scarcely any secrets; and the better the secret, the more scarcely it is kept.

Pard Adams, the fellow who worked for the lumberyard—the same fellow who had replaced our back screen door—was not one to deny the world his opinion as to what he saw and learned in his comings and goings. Pard Adams came and went a lot, and his mouth never stopped running. Neither Ruby nor Booger Red would have hired him in a million years.

Church deacon or not, Bible quoter or not, my mom didn't much like him. She said there was something Catholic about him. She said, "Sometimes, you stand down wind of him, you can catch a whiff of fish and candle."

Now, see, my point is this. When my mom pointed out to Pard Adams the extent to which my dad had repaired, bedamned, and basically excommunicated our back screen door, Pard Adams took it upon himself to begat a legend.

He flat immortalized my dad and his Model T Ford.

You have to remember it was war time. Getting a car was difficult to the point of impossible. New cars? They were just like Lucky Strike cigarettes—gone to war.

Anyway, the point is, we were lucky to have a car at all. That we had one came about in this way: One evening my dad called his aunt and inquired did she still have her Model T Ford. She told him she guessed she did, maybe, down in the barn, likely covered with three acres of chicken poop. She said if he wanted it, and could find it, he was most welcome to it.

We walked over, my dad and I, to the far other end of town, and we found the Model T there in the barn. Three acres of chicken poop was what you might call an underestimation. God only knows what that car had done to offend chickens, but it must have been a felony.

My dad primed the cylinders and cranked. He cranked and primed the cylinders. He told me if there was anything in the world he knew how to handle, it was an automobile. Then he kicked it, just in case. He found a heavy wrench and sort of explained the facts of life to the magneto. Finally, when it still didn't start, he up-turned a bucket and plopped down on it. I knew he was serious. He laid it out plain to that car. He did not leave a crack of space for misunderstanding. He quoted Isaiah, "Produce your cause," he said. "Bring forth your strong reasons!"

My dad was a gentle man, and he knew his Bible. He could quote the Beatitudes from hell to breakfast. He could reel off at least seven of the ten commandants, right off the top of his head. Still and all, he had his limits. If the Beatitudes included "Blessed are the patient," then my dad had forgotten it. The time for talk was over.

He found a rusty ax, laid it across the hood, and

turned the crank once more. That old engine started on the first crank. Started with a lurch and an enthusiastic clamor. If it could have talked, I guess that old engine would have said, "Why didn't *I* think of this?"

We cleared away barrels and bales, hoops and staves, and drove that chicken-poop car home, proud as a couple of twenty dollar bills. My mom took one look and wailed, "I will never be able to show my face in town again!"

Still and all, she did—show her face in town, I mean.

My dad and I cleaned that old car and polished it from up to down. We used toothpicks to scrape out the little cracky places. We admonished off the pieces of straw and the chicken poop, the mud-dauber nests, the scarcely used parts of wooly worms...until, if that car didn't look quite new, it looked next best.

Underneath, we lay on our backs and scraped mud off the front coil springs; mud which my dad said dated back to the Battle of Concord.

I would hazard a gamble that that car was as clean as the marble top of Bernie Klatchmire's soda fountain. My dad polished the wire connections and polished parts around the magneto that I don't guess many people know are even there. He oiled, and he talked earnest. He began to be proud of that car and named it "Lazarus."

While he never outright claimed to be Jesus, going around resurrecting everything that got in his way, he didn't seem to mind when people were amazed at the job he had done on that car. He let them draw their own conclusions.

I will admit to this: I have been steeped and immersed, haphazardly, in religion, but if religion "took" at all with me, it was only to the left of somewhat. I will tell you something else, the two experiences which brought me the closest to being a true believer came from that Model T Ford.

First of all, I came to believe that car was nearly human. Maybe had a heart and soul. Boy, that made me think! I got to where I stepped out the front door instead of the back door to take a leak because, if you are being watched, you can't do it. And I knew that car was watching.

At any rate, my dad used that car to purify the world of one screen door. We talked about it that same evening, sitting by the cistern. He told me that, for the most part, screen doors were a benefit to mankind. He started to tell me about a screen door he remembered from when he was about my age, but the memory seemed to pain him.

He took a long, deep, drag on his cigarette, like he did every time he decided it was time to talk like a father. He wanted me to understand that almost every screen door I would meet in my lifetime would be a *good* screen door. Still, some, he cautioned, and he looked me straight in the eye when he said it, were, "just—regrettably, God's mistakes."

He flicked away his cigarette, shook his head, and started toward the house. Maybe wondering: if there is a God, then how do you explain screen doors?

It's a terrible thing to be old enough to know wisdom when you hear it and know you are still too young to understand it.

So this is the way it was: Pard Adams of the lumber yard had pretty much immortalized my dad. Established his reputation as a fellow you didn't want to mess with if you were a screen door. If there were any screen doors in Epic that felt the urge to be belligerent when my dad was around, I would be very much surprised. No, sir, there was likely not a screen door in

Epic that didn't clinch up its butt when my dad drove by in his Model T.

26

Thursday evening we were on the front porch, my mom sitting upwind of my dad because he was smoking the cigar he had received free and *per gratis* because he had paid the bill at the grocery store. She said she hoped to goodness nobody came by and smelled that thing because, if they did, she would never again be able to show her face in town.

We sat there, my dad and I, grinning out into the coming dark. The taste of my mom's fried raspberry sandwiches was still on our lips. Still there in the mouth corners. Still there if you knew how to work your tongue. Grinning, knowing that heaven could never be better than this, unless God could figure a way to get rid of those seeds, which stuck between the teeth. The cicadas were starting to warm up, and they didn't sound friendly. They sounded like Pygmies building up the fire to roast a Leprechaun.

My mom waved away the cigar smoke with her hand, and reminded us, not that we had been offered the option of forgetfulness, that she would never be able to show her face in town again. God help me if you ever mention this to my mom, but the truth of the matter is, I have never noticed long lines of people waiting for my mom to show her face in town.

But I was mostly watching the lightning bugs. My dad could scarcely keep them away from the glow of his cigar. Maybe it seemed to offer more promise than anything else they were likely to find in Epic on a Thursday evening. My dad explained it as "Ambition."

Mew Washington, Mose's wife, was suddenly there on the sidewalk, bright green turban and all, sporting a few feathers, but a discouraged few. Her face looked as wrinkled as God's first dollar bill. She was right up to the porch before I saw her. Without preamble or damn your eyes, right by the snow-on-the-mountain and near where the jonquils had been in earlier days. Like dandelion fluff she showed up, looking ready to be gone with the first unkind wind. "Appeared," as you might say. But the way she stood, feet wide apart, jungle eyes, she was not about to blow away. She gave me a glance and as near a smile, I guess, as she could manage.

Still and all, if ever there was ever a sad spectacle to behold, it was Mew. I had never before seen her look scared. Mew was the person I would have thought of first did I need the end of a railroad spike bit off. She would have just bitten it off like it was something she did three times a day and said, "There you are. Now looky here at what I got in the oven."

She looked hard into my dad's eyes and didn't blink. "Mose is took bad," she said, "I can't seem to help him."

In my mind I could see old Mose huddled on his bed, packed around with bright feathers and sea shells and smoke that made you wonder. It tightened my belly.

My dad looked her right back. "We'll get the Doctor," he told her.

"New doctor don't do Negroes," Mew said, "Old doctor did; he's dead."

My dad's face took on the same look as when he had killed the screen door and rendered it unto oblivion. He said words which you will not ever hear in the Doxology, even on a slow day in church.

Now, see, I knew the words he used when he adjusted the bands on the car's transmission. But these were words I had never heard him use. I was surprised he knew these words. And I felt sinful because I figured he had learned them from me. I practiced them behind the barn on a regular basis. He must have overheard me. Still yet and all, he had likely been behind more barns than I. It made me wonder.

"Wally," he told me, "Help Mew into the back seat of the car, and get in your self."

I don't believe my dad believed in the devil, so I don't believe he had made any kind of a pact with him concerning that car. No, if my dad had made any pact or commitment, it had been with that old Ford itself. It started on the first crank, and it started moving before my dad got his door closed.

Dr. Benson was a small, prissy man. He looked seriously choked by a necktie that must have been Baptist in origin. Tiny feet and tiny eyes. His squeezy shoes hurt me to look at. I didn't like him. Not by a far cry would I have ever loaned him my BB gun, even to shoot a snake. He was the kind of man that makes a dog give out those deep, gurgle-growl noises, not yet biting, but dang willing. He had only been in Epic since a couple of years before I was born. Maybe fifteen, sixteen years in all, so he still was, as you might say, "suspect."

My dad drove right up onto the yard grass, which he would never have done had things been normal. But things weren't normal. The Model T showed every desire to just go ahead and climb the porch steps and break dishes in the kitchen, but my dad said, "Stay, girl, stay."

He left the engine running, and I was right behind him when he pounded on the door. Dr. Benson allowed the door only somewhat open, and my dad did not give him time to belch nor hiccup. He flat explained the situation. He said, "Grab your bag!"

Dr. Benson glanced out and saw Mew sitting in the Model T and pulled on a sorrowful sad face. Like, maybe an angel who had just busted the E string on his heavenly harp. He told my dad that he did not treat Negroes.

That's when it happened, my second Ford religious experience. That old Model T backfired three times. And those three times came likely quicker and louder than would have been recommended by Henry Ford. You had to be there to understand. I'm not talking about three little bangs, not little nose blows, not little firecracker explosions, not even crack-of-doom booms. No, sir, I will tell you this: the genius of Henry Ford had achieved a sound which, likely, made God want to retool his thunder and reexamine Mr. Ford's patent rights. Maybe God might send old Moses back up the mountain to await further instructions in regard to noise-making. Maybe put an asterisk at the bottom of the Ten Commandments.

The screen door was the first to respond. It swung open, then closed itself gently, politely, without squeak or scrape. With an urge to please not often seen in screen doors, it opened again, without the touch of human hand. See, I figure it this way, screen doors are a lot like people, they have heard the Word but they are waiting for a Sign. This was, flat out, a "born again" screen door. It had heard the Word, and the Word was: watch out for Wilson Gant!

The doctor, and I mean no disrespect, was a little slower to grasp the gravity of the situation than was his screen door. But, when the color returned to his face, he said, "I'll get my bag."

No doubt in my mind, Doctor Benson had never before been in a house quite like that of Mose and Mew. Never before had been in a house filled with bright feathers and rocks and sea shells. Never before smelled that smoke, because I doubt that smoke-smell is taught at where you learn to be a doctor. He had never before been so close to the blessings of God as to smell oven smells that would just melt your teeth. In point of fact, as the fellow says, he would have never have entered that house, except that when my dad turned the key off, the Model T did not choose to participate. It kept running...explaining....

Mew was just a step or two behind me. Anxious and worried as she was, she stopped and picked up a cardinal feather, that I had stepped over without seeing. She laid it atop the hood of that car. It did not ruffle; it did not blow off. I watched, and I thought.

Doctor Benson fiddled and fussed over Mose, making doctor sounds from his throat. In the end, about all he did was give Mew a little jar of salve to rub on Mose's chest. When we dropped the Doctor off at his house, my dad placed some folded money in his hand.

That night I dreamed. I didn't dream of Mose. I didn't dream of Dr. Benson nor the Model T. I dreamed of Loris Admuson, the albingo girl. I dreamed she was standing in some sort of a fuzzy place, maybe a place with barns and flowers, maybe some hollyhocks around and, maybe, some potato vines. She was looking at me with those deep-strange eyes, those eyes which didn't seem to have a behind to them. Just looking at me. In my dream I sat astraddle my bicycle, my foot on the right pedal, on the up side, ready for a hard push down, ready to escape. I was praying: "Sweet Jesus, please tell me one more time and I will try to remember: what is six times six?"

27

On my new job I mostly scrubbed and cleaned. Ruby was a stickler for clean, especially in the Moon Butter room. Every day Mr. Strang and I worked the route. We drove all around Epic, picking up empty bottles, leaving off full ones. Then we would head south, picking up Deep Shaft, leaving off Moon Butter. The route was the easy part. The hard part was coming back and facing that pile of bottles and pans waiting to be boiled and dried.

But that first day is the one I mostly remember. Ruby got home from Armageddon just after dark. I was so hungry my belly growled. At least I didn't have to worry about my mom fretting about me. She knew I was amongst milk, and therefore, learning responsibility.

Ruby had borrowed a car from someone. I remember those headlights jouncing up the lane. One time they'd be shining toward the center of the earth, then, quicker than you could dunk a donut, they pointed near straight up.

The shot-out windows of Booger Red's Emporium had already been boarded up. She reported to Mr. Strang and me that in all her mortal life she had never seen so many guns. They were stuck in belts or held in hands, not hidden. People leaning against light poles and in doorways around the Emporium. She said, "I swear and be damned, you could walk through the Colt and Winchester factories, both together, and never see so many guns." She said it was more than your life was worth to just walk down the street if you were a Chicago Hot Shot or even if you were just wearing pointy-toed shoes. I could understand what she meant about being more than your life was worth, because that is what my dad always said about the way my mom cooked liver.

Ruby said it was one thing to steal the Catholic church (like they sometimes did in Armageddon), probably not really right, but still—and it was just a joke to steal the jail. But to desecrate Booger Red's Emporium was beyond the unbelievable.

Ruby said Booger Red had been thinking about putting in a pool table. She said that in Armageddon, if you rolled a Catholic church and a jail into one grand chunk and put it on the town square with electric lights and a fountain squirting out lemonade, it would not draw as many people as a pool table in Booger Red's Emporium. She concluded that the citizens of Armageddon were just not going to take much more guff from those Chicago people with their pointy shoes.

Ruby was not in a good mood, but she checked the pans and bottles I had scrubbed, and satisfied me a smile. I had started some potatoes frying and started some pork chops to burning. Ruby more or less depleted herself into her personal chair at the kitchen table and, from its moan I figured, given the option, it would have rather been a cedar chest, or even firewood.

I had the plates and silverware already out and also the sugar bowl, although there was not a thing on God's green earth on that table that might need sugar. Still and all, that sugar bowl added a touch of elegance and, at least in my mind, we were a little short of elegance. And heck, for all I knew, maybe half the people in the world might vastly prefer sugar on their fried potatoes and pork chops. Well, I placed that food on the table in front of Ruby and she looked at it and then she looked at me, and then she looked back at the food. Then she said, "My God!" I took that as a good sign. Then Mr. Strang came in from the barn and sat down, looked at my food, and said, "Jesus Christ!" Neither of them were usually praying people. Still and all, I couldn't help grinning, inside, when they offered that blessing. It wasn't exactly the way my granddad usually said his eating blessing, but, still and all, this was the first meal I had ever cooked. Likely blessings varied from meal to meal.

I started home, deep-knowing I was guilty; but four miles happy. I was guilty of the sin of pride. Beaming. Out loud I said: "Sweet Jesus, I thank you for helping me provide that supplement for Ruby and Mr. Strang.

"For the strength of their souls and bodies," I added. I shouted the words because I had just remembered them and figured that they needed to be included if people's souls and bodies were going to be considered by Jesus. The Strangs had had a hard day.

Even knowing that Jesus had been spear-stabbed in the side and not in the ear, I shouted. You can't be too careful.

I tried to remember other prayer words. "Trespasses," bore down on my mind, so I said that several times. "Leviticus" seemed to ring a bell, so I threw that in a time or two. It couldn't hurt. Then I said "Amen," because that's what you say when you are finished talking to Jesus.

I have stopped being offended that he never responds. To tell you the truth, if the clouds ever parted and Jesus hollered "Amen" back at me, I would likely get a nose bleed.

Had I been more than a half block away from home I might have tried to work in some Beatitudes, but I'll tell you this: those "Blessed are those's" are nearly as many as the "Begats," and if you tried to work them all into a prayer, you would likely just wake up in the morning and find the world either asleep or plumb gone.

See, for a while I was interested in begats. I would hear my mother and my aunts talking about begats. They would be basting the goose, or adding little marsh-mallows to the sweet potatoes. They never outright *said* "begat," but I knew that was what they were talking about. You just don't giggle and whisper that much if you are not talking about begats.

So I said "Amen" to Jesus. Then, to myself, out loud, I said, "If there is another boy in the world who could have fixed a better supper, I would be very much surprised."

On my way home a freight train let out one of those loud whistles that must have been designed to scare the people down in Cuba. It sounded right by my ear. Without a thought, I moved to the side of that gravel road. You don't want to mess with a freight train. See, I had lived all my life only a potato patch away from the railroad. I had never seen a train on a gravel road before, but like I said, you don't want to mess with a freight train.

Purdy Grundy was standing in front of our house with a smile on his face. It was bad of me, but I turned off, down through the tomato patch. I found the biggest, most ripe tomato I could see and kicked it in a very unchristian way. Then I found it again and stomped on it. I had had a hard day too, and I wasn't up to having another fight with Purdy. Purdy didn't ask and it didn't occur to me to explain why I smashed a tomato. Some days, the pleasure of kicking the hell out of a tomato is the best you can hope for. But Purdy was there and I guess I was glad. We didn't talk about steamboats and we most sure did not talk about Loris Admuson. Mostly, we just stood and kicked chunks of gravel by way of apology to each other.

It was good to be friends again, but I was not sorry when Purdy left. Besides having my chores to do, I needed to compare the Sears and Roebuck ladies with the Montgomery-Ward ladies—what you might call, *"feminine apparel* wise." There wasn't an albingo in the bunch, so I had to guess. Even looking at her sideways, Loris was, at best, a double-ought zero when it came to "cup size." As near as I could figure Loris didn't even have a cup size. On a good day she maybe would have qualified for a Tablespoon.

28

Next morning, on the way to the dairy, I picked up two good-sized pieces of gravel. When I got close enough to those goats, I flung them each one apiece, without prejudice—and missed both times. As the goats mostly did, unless they caught me unexpected, they chose to ignore my presence. Never mind that I had spent half my life feeding them and providing them with water. Never mind my saintly restraint in not kicking them more than I did.

I didn't get halfway near the dairy before I was announced.

That old black crow.

Ruby called it "The Company Crow," because it was always loyal and protective of the Strang Dairy. Sometimes she fired her .22 rifle in its general direction just to keep it awake, but she would rather have chopped her arm off than hit it. I don't claim to know bird talk, but I know what it was hollering back on those occasions: "You fat human! You couldn't tune a guitar with both hands tied behind you!"

See, Ruby had some strange friends. I don't know, maybe I was one of them. That crow was one for sure. I'll tell you this: had I come with evil intent toward Ruby, I wouldn't have wanted that crow between us.

I am sure there was no negotiated agreement between them. The crow simply saw a need and filled it. It seemed to work.

When I came in the door Ruby gave me the best smile she could muster. I guess I've seen better smiles on tombstones than the one Ruby gave me. She had a lot of bad on her mind. Still and all, the first thing she said to me was, "How's Mose Washington?" I told her Mose was feeling better, his knot hole abscess was healing, and he was getting around some. She set out some Moon Butter, a pint of Deep Shaft and a half pint of Blind Sorrow for me to take to him. She told me to be careful not to spill any Blind Sorrow on my clothes or bicycle. She told me to warn Mew that Blind Sorrow should only be used in case of imminent death or to fertilize cactus.

I had just asked what was special about Blind Sorrow when Mr. Strang came in. He came in cursing goats back to Noah's Ark, and his own goats in particular. Before you could blink, he picked up a half pint and took an unbelievable swig. He wheezed and shook his head and explained to me that Blind Sorrow was made mostly from ground up and fermented alligator and water moccasin meat.

Ruby snatched the bottle from Mr. Strang.

Later, when I told my dad about Ruby's generosity toward Mose, he said that when she passed away, Ruby would sit at the right hand of God. He mulled on that and decided that God, because of Ruby's broad butt, would likely have to scoot further down the bench and Jesus would have to be moved to a three legged stool. Organizing the seating arrangements in heaven became a problem for my dad. He had not yet decided what to do with the Apostles.

"Apostles!" he muttered to himself. "Why in the world do we need *twelve* Apostles?" My dad was always trying to cut costs, so he started back toward the house having an earnest discussion with himself as to which six Apostles could be laid off without disrupting the world.

At supper he announced that really, we didn't need any Apostles at all. My mother was busy slicing off the burnt side of the fried weenies and seemed to have no opinion as to the necessity of Apostles, but still, she was listening. When my dad asked what had happened to the weenies, she sidestepped the issue with one word, "Archangels?"

"Archangels!" My dad repeated. I saw his face fall. He had forgotten them. "We'll just have to get them some folding chairs and put them near the back, maybe."

Ruby and I ran the route that day because Mr. Strang was carrying a full load of Blind Sorrow and singing a version of "The Girl I Left Behind Me", that should never be heard by the ears of a Christian.

It was getting late when Ruby and I arrived in Betcherass. The sun was behind us and it glared in my eyes from the windshield, but it didn't seem to bother Ruby. We hadn't been in town two minutes when we learned that Pete Ziotky's load of booze had been hijacked.

When Ruby heard about the hijacking I was near mortified by my own personal ineptitude at cussing. It's a wonder I didn't swear off altogether.

A fellow—Ruby knew him but I didn't—told us that Pete had not been hurt at all in the hijacking, but that he had skinned his knee as he ran through the timber when he felt a sudden and understandable desire to visit his elderly parents in Nebraska.

29

Three days later Ruby was hijacked and kidnapped.

Maybe if Mr. Strang and I had been running the route as usual it wouldn't have happened. But I was sick with what my mom believed was the chicken pox. The doctor said it was just a rash. She slammed the door behind him and explained that if there was anything in the world she knew about it was chicken pox. She said that if I didn't stop scratching my neck, they would have to cut my leg off above the knee.

Mr. Strang's joints were too stiff to run the route by himself, so Ruby worked the route south, driving that old truck toward Armageddon. She was just north of Armageddon when two Chicago Hot Shots forced her off the road and hustled her away.

Even with all of the bad things that had been happening in the Little Balkans, I guess nobody ever gave a thought to anything bad happening to Ruby. No, sir, it was much more likely that Ruby would "happen bad" on somebody else.

Ace Williams likely broke all land-speed records to bring in the news. He had seen the incident from what he called "too far away to help," and his teeth were still chattering. I didn't know whether to puke or cry, so I did both.

I will tell you this: when the news spread, lots of the men and some of the women of Buffalo County headed south—carrying guns and pitchforks and whiffletrees and whatever came to hand. My own dad wanted to go, but his favored weapon was a cudgel. He spent all afternoon going from one store to the next inquiring did they carry cudgels, but all in vain. He told me it was a sad old day when a fellow couldn't find a single cudgel in a town the size of Epic. I had never seen him look so downcast. But even without my dad to encourage the mob with a cudgel, tempers were hot and dangerous. If you had a third cousin who even knew how to spell the word "Chicago," your life was in peril.

But nobody had any idea where they might find Ruby. Even as large as she was, there were, unfortunately, plenty of places to hide her. No question about it, they would take the Moon Butter she was hauling. That was more or less expected and just a hazard of the trade. What they really wanted from Ruby was her secret recipe for making Moon Butter.

You had to know Ruby to understand the ambitiousness of those rascals. On the outside she looked just as soft as a feather bed. On the inside she was made of mule skin and pig iron. I knew there weren't enough pry bars in Buffalo County to open Ruby's mouth did she happen to be inclined otherwise.

It was late in the afternoon of the third day when Ruby drove that old truck up the driveway. Her face was somewhat bruised, and she sported a black eye that anyone could be proud of, but she was smiling. I will never forget the hug she gave me. She even gave a hug to Mr. Strang, but not as enthusiastic as the one she gave me. She had not divulged the secret of Moon Butter. What she had divulged was her ability to use her knee in such a manner that the fat Chicago man would likely never be able to stand straight again. And, for sure, he'd never be able to increase the population on the planet Earth.

She had tripped that skinny Chicago man and placed her foot on the back of his neck until he begged to see his mother one more time before he died. Begging didn't work. Somewhere in Chicago, a mother waits in vain for her son. You had to see Ruby's feet to understand. Ruby said she hadn't meant to burn the hideout. It had been a pure accident. She said she had just rubbed those two hoodlums together like a Boy Scout would two sticks— and they had "just become overhet."

No one bothered with a serious inquest concerning the dead one. My dad looked up the record, and it said: "Suicide: death caused by leaving Chicago." See, down here we have an abundance of two things: booze and common sense. It did not take a genius to recognize that Ruby did not take a train or bus to Chicago to step on that dumb sucker's neck. If you can find more justice anyplace on God's green earth than in Buffalo County, I would be very much surprised.

It got quieter for a while after that. There were still Chicago thugs around, of course, and more thugs would come.

30

During those days I had not forgotten Mose Washington. All those bad days, God awful bad, bad days. There was some shooting and cutting a few miles south. Some booze stolen and some poured out on the ground by the Law. Some stills smashed and piled up in front of the court house to prove that God was on the side of the Law. Ruby said times were awful hard for the business. But the people with whom I mingled did not seem to hold a grudge against God. He let enough Deep Shaft slip by to allow families to buy groceries on a regular basis.

Mose was doing well. Mew had pounded a cork into his knot hole and tied feathers on the part of the cork that would not go in. Around the cork she had smeared a goo that smelled like a mixture of 'coon piss and peanut brittle.

Mew allowed him one teaspoon of Blind Sorrow each day. She told me that she had started with two teaspoons but that had caused twigs and green leaves to form on his wooden leg. Mew had what some might consider unusual tastes, but having a husband with leaves on his leg was not one of them. There was also the possibility of attracting squirrels, and Mew said she would not live with a man who had a winter supply of acorns rattling around in his leg.

I admit to seeing Loris somewhat often. One day she showed me a scab on her knee and it seemed sort of sacred, like something maybe I should not know about. She let me touch it. My God, I touched her knee!

I just don't guess old Purdy Grundy ever touched that scab!

The time came when I wanted Loris to meet Mose and Mew. I wanted her to meet Ruby, too; but what with the black eye and all, Ruby was not, as you might say, "presentable."

Loris's absolute whiteness maybe bothered Mose a little at first. But Mose's absolute blackness didn't seem to bother Loris. Mew and Loris took up like a barn afire. They were friends from the first, and I was glad. Mew led Loris into the house. I stayed on the porch with Mose.

My dad always claimed Mew was a Voodoo Queen. He didn't say that against her. What was, just was. So Mose and I sat on the porch, and he told me about the time a water moccasin almost bit him. But that was when he had both legs, and he said there wasn't a snake in the world could catch him when he had both legs. He said one might possibly catch him now because he had slowed down some.

All that talk about snakes and the treatment for bites reminded me that Loris and I had brought Mose a little gift. Loris's father had worked in the office at one of the mines, Camp 24, until the mine closed down. Then, like everybody else, he had to find a new way to support his family. His solution was called "Null and Void," and many people, when they tasted it, considered it a tragedy that he had wasted so many years working at a mine. Anyway, our gift to Mose was a small jar of Null and Void. Loris had snitched it, but her dad, even though he was of Scandinavian descent, had a good heart and would not have begrudged it.

I had waited until Mew was busy showing Loris the secret things that were spread around the house: bones, feathers, and things you didn't even want to know what were. Then I pulled the jar of Null and Void out from my overalls. Mose's face broke into that old wrinkledy-crackledy smile as he unscrewed the lid and smelled it deep.

"You're a good boy, Wally," he told me. He told me that so often I was tempted to believe him. Had my mom known I was walking around Epic with an albingo girl and had a jar of Null and Void hidden in my overalls, she would have called me a *bad* boy. To tell the truth, that would have been the nicest thing she would have called me.

Anyway, Mose took two long pulls from that jar and settled back, comfortable.

I will tell you this: sometimes it is hard to know if you are improving the world or making it worse. And there is nothing in the Bible concerning Null and Void. Such divine guidance might help a fellow choose the proper path. Still and all, sometimes you just *know*. When Mose found the bottom of that jar of Null and Void, he stood up and stomped his wooden leg on the porch floor and hollered in his crackledy voice, "Bring on those goddamn water moccasins!"

On the way home Loris and I stopped at the slough to look down and see if we could spot any water snakes. Then I forgot about snakes. What I saw, mirrored up from the water, was Loris's white, white face. It jarred me some because I had plumb forgotten that she was an albingo. She was as much too white as Mose was too black. Not having any better sense, I blurted out what was on my mind, "How come you're an albingo?"

She didn't take a swing at me as, maybe, she should have. She just laughed. *"Albino,"* she said, "Not albingo."

I guess it wasn't the first time she had heard the question. "My dad says I'm albino because God already had a plethora of angels."

Now, see, maybe that would have cleared things right up for some people, but I wasn't among the chosen. I enlarged on my misdemeanor by honestly and straightforwardly admitting that I didn't know much about angels but, if God's angels had caught the plethora, it seemed to me that He should be able to clear it right up. She laughed at me again, and I felt as foolish as a fellow who couldn't remember six times six.

That was when I discovered that Loris would likely end up being a school teacher. She explained to me that "plethora" wasn't something you caught, like maybe the measles. Her dad had told her, "The word 'plethora' just means you have too many angels." There didn't seem to be any doubt in her mind but what her dad knew all anybody would ever need to know about God, angels, plethoras, and albinos.

According to her dad, one day God was sitting around whittling out one angel after another, when a thought struck him: Why am I doing this? Every time I make another angel I just have to build another ivory palace!

So, right then and there, He quit. Instead, He sent Loris down to earth as a baby girl. Her whiteness just proved that she had some angel blood in her. According to Loris's dad, God then turned His hand to whittling porcupines, which do not have wings that break off just when you think you've got them about right—and do not require ivory palaces.

Loris was part angel, and I was not surprised.

31

It was soon after Ruby gave me my first glimpse of the Moon Butter room when I discovered my mistake. What I had mistook for a shadowy fence post with a black beard was really Howard, Ruby's draft-dodging brother. Still and all, I hold myself irresponsible, because a better man than I would have made the same mistake.

Maybe even the G-men, who sometimes came around trying to catch Howard, had actually looked right at him and wondered just why in the world anyone would hang a black beard on a fence post.

That day Ruby dragged Howard out from a dark corner, dusted him off a little, and explained him to me. I swear and be damned, if anyone ever needed explaining, it was bearded and barefoot Howard. She asked then, did I remember the oath I had sworn concerning the secrets of the Strang Dairy. Of course I did, but it crossed my mind that if Howard was one of those secrets, I still might owe her another oath or two.

Ruby gave me the whole story. She said the reason Howard had forgone the pleasures of the military life was a matter of aversions. Howard was averse to bugles, sergeants, tents, and any number of other things. But, the main thing he aversed was having his butt blown off.

Ruby was plainly at a loss as to what plans, if any, Howard had made in regard to protecting his butt. But she figured until he made up his mind, the Moon Butter room was the safest place in Buffalo County to hide it.

Keeping secrets about the Moon Butter was no problem for me; I plain didn't know any. Keeping the secret of Howard was different. Secrets are about as heavy a burden to lay on a boy as is a group of goats. I knew my dad would give up his old-age pension to hear about Howard. And my mom would say, "Poor Ruby! She'll never be able to show her face in town." Mose would get a chuckle over white boys outsmarting each other.

Of course, even if allowed, I wouldn't have told Loris. Girls can't keep a secret for snap.

On the days Ruby made Moon Butter, Howard and I worked together cleaning the pots and pans. Howard always worked with his back right against the wall protecting that which he held most dear. He had to. Although Ruby took the making of Moon Butter dead serious—given the opportunity, she would give him a good goosing and holler, "BANG." That meant Howard would be spending the rest of the day hiding among the sunflowers, and I would do all the work.

The arrival of the goats was maybe the happiest day of Howard's life. And though they didn't realize it at the time, it was maybe the happiest day of the goats' lives too. By the end of the first day, what bloom there might have been on the rose of goat ownership had faded for Mr. Strang.

In my heart of hearts, as you might say, I had waited for the time when Mr. Strang would humbly ask me for the most effective words to use in dealing with goats, should a fellow ever be so unfortunate as to have goats. I knew I could give him a rare selection and, I knew I would, if asked, even though it might destroy any illusions he had about my coming from a Christian home.

The truth is, I had woefully underestimated Mr. Strang. Either he had been blessed with a God given talent, or he had owned goats in a previous life. By the end of the first day I had lost most of my vain-glorious pride and would not have dared to offer any help at all in the art of goat-cussery. By the end of the second day, if Mr. Strang was with the goats, I was taking the long way around, for fear someone would see me blushing.

But old Howard took to those goats like they were favorite cousins. He could only go out to the pen when it was too dark for the G-men to spot him and too dark for anyone to try to blow his butt off, but he went every night. And friendship blossomed. It blossomed to the point that Howard soon took complete charge of the care and handling of "Lefty" and "Righty" which is what he named them. Mr. Strang was more than happy to give the goats over to Howard. Still and all, he reminded me, "We are judged by the company we keep." After Howard and the goats became friends, Mr. Strang admitted to having lost a little of his respect for the goats.

Towards the end of that first week, as I was about to leave for home, Mr. Strang told me if I wanted to see a sight and a half, I should come back after dark. Well, come time, he and Ruby and I walked down to the goat pen, and what I saw was a regular circus. Howard had trained those goats to do more tricks than you could ever imagine. They could roll over and play dead, jump through hoops, and stand balanced on each other's backs. Ruby was proud as could be and told me that Howard could have trained them to jump through *burning* hoops except the light would have just been an invitation for someone to blow his butt off.

Mr. Strang bemoaned that those goats could have made him a wealthy man; but because of his stupid brother-in-law, they would only perform in the dark of night. The *piece of resistance*, as you might say, was when Howard had the goats add simple numbers by tapping their hooves on a board. There is nothing more sickening than a show-off goat!

That night I dreamed they had learned six times six, and Loris had cast me away like an old shoe.

32

As much as I liked working for Mr. Strang and Ruby, some days, when my back was aching from washing Moon Butter utensils, I looked back on the happy, care-free days of my childhood. Sometimes I thought about my foolish dreams of singing "Carry Me Back to Old Virginny" on WIBW or playing a silver cornet in the Fourth of July parade. Late afternoons when my back was aching worse than any canebrake slave could ever dream of, I could almost hear the distant toot of a steam-boat coming for to carry me home.

I guess I was sort of in that frame of mind when Ruby emerged her head from the Moon Butter room and declared, "It's too quiet!" Now, see, after being exposed to what seemed to be the normal side of our business— namely and to wit: murder, hijacking, kidnapping and the finding of an occasional cockroach on a kitchen table—quiet was a phenomenon I was game to try. But one of Ruby's knacks was telling the difference between *quiet* and *too quiet*. And Ruby was right.

About two o'clock the next morning, Howard, without

a by-your-leave or a damn-your-eyes, landed in the bed right between herself and Mr. Strang. He was screaming that he had heard gunshots and somebody was trying to blow his butt off.

Mr. Strang asked if that had indeed happened, and Howard said, "No." Mr. Strang said by grab he would soon rectify that himself. Mr. Strang said brother-in-law or no brother-in-law, he did not intend to share his bed with Howard. He had never become accustomed to sleeping with anyone with a beard and skinny ankles, and such a possibility had not been mentioned in his marriage vows. Ruby said Howard had taken umbrage at the snipe concerning his skinny ankles and protested strongly. Whereupon Mr. Strang had declared that, by God, tomorrow he was going to call Camp Leonard Wood and have the soldiers come get Howard and blow his butt off. He would also inquire their opinion concerning skinny ankles.

It was not until morning that they found Ruby's friend, the watch-crow, lying at the front door. Its wing had been broken by a blast of birdshot, and Ruby said she didn't know how under the light of the living sun it had been able to get to the front door. She said the shooting was no accident. She said nobody went out shooting crows at two o'clock in the morning except for one good reason, and that good reason was to silence the best watch-crow that ever lived so they could sneak up and steal the Moon Butter recipe.

By the time I got there, Ruby had laid the shot-crow in her own bed, and Mr. Strang was uselessly explaining that he had not been raised in a family where a fellow was expected to sleep in the same bed with brothers-in-law and crows.

Not knowing what else to do, she had melted some Moon Butter and used an eye dropper to stoke that crow up until she thought she had seen it grin a little. Still and all, there wasn't much she could do, and the future looked bleak for the crow. Out of its sight Ruby had started sewing black armbands for us to wear in case worse came to worst.

There was no question of Ruby leaving that crow alone in its misery. And yet, the dairy work had to be done. Ruby needed to be producing Moon Butter and Mr. Strang milk and fill bottles. Then he and I would run the route. It was my own good idea to ask Loris to sit with and care for the crow. Since Ruby hadn't met Loris, she wasn't sure about my idea. So I mentioned that Loris almost became an angel but became an albino instead. Mr. Strang, who was a little grumpy for want of a good night's sleep, asked the obvious and reasonable question as to why she had not gone ahead and become an angel. I told him that God had simply got tired of whittling. I guess that satisfied him because he just said "Judas Priest," and went off to the barn.

Loris looked to be a first class bird nurse. She and Ruby hit it off from the start and Ruby went out to the Moon Butter room with some of the heavy load lifted off her heart.

Running the route went pretty much per usual that day, with that pleasant boredom that gave us the chance to complain about being bored. One thing was different: before we started driving south as we always did, we drove north, toward the town of Less.

Mr. Strang told me that when the pioneers settled there, it was more or less what they had hoped to find. "But," he said, "what with the bitching wives and the squalling children, the optimistic pioneer sprit of the founding fathers had worn pretty thin. Some said 'It's good enough,' but the majority echoed back, 'More or

Less.' So on the early maps that's how you'll find it—
More or Less, Kansas."

It stayed that way, More or Less, until a strong wind
came and blew down the oldest tree in town. It was a
Cottonwood, and some judged it might be as much as
four years old. Anyway, with the loss of that tree, Mr.
Strang said the citizens lost some of their hubris. If
asked the name of their town, even the old die-hards
would just stare at the ground and say, "Less."

There were still a few rambledy-shack, embarrassed-
looking buildings strung out along Only street, and Mr.
Strang pointed out as to where the wooden fire hydrant
had stood before it burnt down. We parked in front of
the church, right in front of the sign which said:

Welcome to The Kingdom of God
—Beware the Dog

The reason for the dog was that someone had stolen
the lightning rod off the steeple and something had to be
done. The ladder the thief had used was still there, leaning against the building as a testimony to the honesty of
the citizens of Less, Kansas, and as a testimony to the
fact that, now that the lightning rod was gone, there
wasn't much above ground worth stealing.

The new preacher, Reverend Claude Applehanz, had,
in a snit, transferred to Less from East Armageddon
when the City Council voted five to zero to convert the
church into a whorehouse. He was glad to see us
because he had heard from other preachers in the Little
Balkans that church attendance rose an average of sev-
enty-three percent when they spread Ruby's Moon
Butter on their communion wafers. The only problem
being that some folks felt the compelling need to receive
the sacrament at odd hours—like the middle of the
night—and many requested "seconds," just to be sure
they were right with the Lord. Leave it to good old Ruby

to send the Reverend a *per gratis* sample for the betterment of the world.

From Less we headed back south. I watched the miles roll by with a smile on my face because, there was no getting around it, I had helped make the world a better place. Like it or not, the sinners of Less, Kansas, were about to slide into the arms of Jesus on a Moon-Butter-greased path through the help and abetment of yours truly, Wally Gant.

We passed through Epic and made our usual stops: Galenaville, Cedar Rump, I'llbedamned, Betcherass, and North Dinglebutt. It was business as usual: picking up a little Deep Shaft here, dropping off a little Moon Butter there. It was away past suppertime when we got back to the dairy. Rain clouds were moving in from the west, and the woe-be-tide at the dairy was so thick you could near sop it up with a sponge.

Loris had gone home, and Ruby rocked alone beside the sickbed. The crow had shown some signs of making a rally earlier, but at about a quarter to five it had spasmed into a relapse. Ruby said the end was near.

I picked up a spasmed-off crow feather and left on the run to get Mew.

33

I was still more than half a block from Mew's house when I spotted her running toward me like the Devil was on her tail. "Give me the feather, Wally!" she hollered. How she knew I was carrying a crow-spasmed feather I will likely never know, but if it wasn't some of her Voodoo Queen magic, I would be very much surprised.

I laid that little black feather in the palm of her hand, and she rubbed her bony finger over it, soft. "May be too late," she told me.

Mew didn't waste time on what you might call friendly amenities. She was moving off like a mail train when she called back for me to ask my dad to bring his car and pick up Mose and her gunnysack.

Now, at the risk of making myself appear a bad person and a poor friend, I will admit that making another breath-snatching, side-ache run for a sick crow was not high on my list of desires. Still and all, it seemed to be my responsibility. Maybe my mom was right about milk causing responsibility in a boy. I didn't have time to dwell on it right then, but it crossed my mind that nobody else in Epic seemed to be grinding their feet off on the dad-blamed sidewalk in the name of responsibility. Heck no, as far as they were concerned all the crows in the world could wither and die untimely and unremorsed deaths.

The upshot, of course, was that I slammed one responsible foot in front of the other responsible foot as fast as a fellow has ever done in this world. If I died, never mind. My best hope was that my mom would place *"Died from too much milk, and of such is the kingdom of Heaven"* on my lonely tombstone.

There are, most likely, more people than not who would poke fun at anybody who believes in the power of a Voodoo Queen. I'm not saying if I do or if I don't. All I am saying is, when I got home the car engine was running and my dad was sitting behind the steering wheel with a look on his face that showed he had no idea as to where or why he might be going. Another thing, we found Mose waiting for us, Mew's gunnysack doctor bag in one hand and a two-barrel shotgun in the other.

I'm not putting Alexander Graham Bell down in any way, shape, nor form, but I found some smugness in knowing that Mew could communicate, too, and without wires or batteries.

I guess the kindest I can say about the headlamps of our Model T Ford is that they tried. My dad, who loved that car, was only bragging somewhat when he claimed that on a clear night with a full moon, he could tell a cowshed from a school teacher at twenty feet. It was, as I saw it, what they call a moot point, because it took the brakes at least twenty-five feet to stop the car. In all fairness, I will admit that, in my remembrance, my dad never ran over either a school teacher nor a cowshed. Anyway, such being the case, our front bumper was straining against the red-tile wall of the Strang Dairy before my dad proclaimed that we had arrived. Seen in the yellow light of those headlamps it was a mighty gloomy place, and, if a fellow happened to be a shot crow, he couldn't have picked a more appropriate place to die.

I was the first one out of the car so I held Mose's shotgun while he untangled his wooden leg and anticipated his way through the car door. See, Mose was the kind of fellow who never forgot when a kindness was done to him. And he would never in a million years forget Ruby's kindness in supplying him, *per gratis,* the only balm that could ease the pain of his abscessed knothole.

So Mose had brought his shotgun along for company while he sat in the evening dews and damps. Although he was half blind he filled in for the wounded guard-crow. Howard, who had a deep and abiding ability to spot anyone carrying a gun, clamped his endangered butt tight against the red-tile wall, no doubt in my mind, ready to keep it there through the falling leaves of autumn and the snows of winter if necessary. But it wasn't necessary. Mose stumped on down to take up his guard position by the road, and if he felt the nudge of any proclivity to blow anything off of Howard, he didn't show it by word or deed.

My dad was scarce through the front door before Mr. Strang collared him. "Wilson," he shouted, "I will *not* sleep in a bed that has been desecrated by crow-sweat and a hairy brother-in-law!" I guess my dad could see the reasonableness of Mr. Strang's feelings, because he didn't offer a word in support of anyone who might try to force such a thing upon Mr. Strang.

I wouldn't have thought it possible, but while I was gone after Mew the guard-crow had taken another turn for the worse. It had developed a chill, and Ruby said,

"The poor thing was shivering so bad it was shaking the whole bed." That accounted for the blankets and throw rugs that were tucked around it until there wasn't much of the crow available to the naked eye. I figured if the "poor thing" was soaking Mr. Strang's bed with sweat no one should be bowled over with surprise.

Mew snatched her voodoo medicine gunnysack doctor bag and emptied it on the bed. She hovered over the bed, placing a sea shell here, a feather there, a bright stone or two right on top of that poor old crow until I don't guess it had room to belch. She crooned, Mew did—just rolled her eyes up into her head and crooned—and I didn't need anybody to tell me that she was far, far away.

It was getting on towards ten o'clock, and my dad had announced several times that he should be getting on home. But about that time Mr. Admuson, Loris's father, came through the door, uninvited. But he was welcome because he was carrying two pint jars of Null and Void. I will say this for my dad, he was never the one to breech the rules of etiquette. And anyone carrying two jars of Null and Void obviously deserved a warm handshake and a little friendly conversation. In point of fact, as a fellow might say, it was a lesson to me to see just how seriously everybody there got down to the business of etiquette.

Now, I've never heard it preached on, but there seemed to be more than politeness involved. Likely there is a parable or two there, somewhere, maybe hidden away in the Book of Micah or Malachi. It would contain something about crow-healing; something about Null and Void. Still, it was plain to see that a sick crow can bring out the best in people. Mr. Strang, who seldom bent his elbow, took a long pull as the first jar went around, and so did Ruby.

My dad offered a toast of good health in the general

direction of the bedridden crow. Then, likely wondering if his heartfelt good wishes might have gone astray before they reached the bed, he tilted the jar again, leaving no doubt in anyone's mind as to exactly which crow and which bed he was good-wishing for. Now see, to the best of my knowledge, my dad had never before known or spoken three words to that crow. Still and all, he proceeded to make it clear that this was the finest, most loyal and hard-working crow God ever placed on this green earth. I had the feeling that he could have said a lot more, but before he had a chance to recommend the crow for president of the United States, Mr. Admuson retrieved the jar.

Mr. Admuson made sure his throat was good and wet before he admitted that there were damn few things he didn't know about nursing sick crows. Mew kept on with her crooning and eye-rolling without seeming to draw a breath or notice that there was anyone else within eleven miles of her.

"Py Colly, in the Old Country you can't walk across the street without tripping over three or four sick crows," Mr. Admuson explained. He sloshed the Null and Void around in the jar, took another swallow, and told us that, in all honesty, on some days you might trip over five or six sick crows. That was the reason he gave for leaving the old country. "Chust tired of nursing dem damn crows!" he said.

Nevertheless and howsoever, he seemed to have one more crow-healing left in him. He filled Ruby's eye-dropper with Null and Void and excused Mew out of the way with his hip. Then he poked a finger into the covers where one might reasonably expect a crow's stomach to be. When the crow opened its beak to burp out an indignation, Mr. Admuson emptied that old eye-dropper right down its gullet.

In the meantime, Mr. Strang had noticed the Null and Void jar sitting lonely and forlorn, and drained the last drops from it. "Wally," he told me, "I can never sleep in that bed again! That bed has brought me rest and comfort, and I had looked forward to dying in it. But now it has been desecrated beyond redemption!" I had never before seen Mr. Strang cry, but tears were rolling down his cheeks. "My own bed," he groaned. "And before the cock crows three times, I must take that bed out and burn it.

"You're a good boy, Wally. You're the best boy I ever saw, and I will whip any man who says otherwise. Wilson," he hollered at my dad, "Wally is the best boy I ever saw, and I will whip any man who says otherwise!"

"Walnut!" My dad corrected, a little too loudly. "When he was born, his mother wanted to name him Walnut!"

"My own bed! Forever rendered unfit for human habitation by man or beast!"

"I will whip any man who says his mother didn't want to name him Walnut!" my dad guaranteed.

Ruby had moved from the rocking chair to a chair without arms because she had started writing a song called "Woe Betide the Sonofabitch Who Shot My Crow," in A-minor, and it is difficult to do A-minor with arms on your chair.

"Walnut," Mr. Strang vowed, "tomorrow you and I will go out and buy a new bed. And God help anybody...." Mr. Strang's voice trailed off. He grabbed an old envelope and a pencil and started writing. I looked over his shoulder. He was making a list of people and things which would only be found on his new bed after his dead body had been stomped into powder:

1. Brothers-in-law (hairy or unhairy)
2. Crows (sweaty or unsweaty)
3. Sea shells, feathers and stones

4. Voodoo crooning
5. Acorns
6. Snakes or worms
7. Fever blisters

Now, in all honesty, I had never personally witnessed an acorn nor a snake, worm, or fever blister on Mr. Strang's bed. But I figured he realized he had taken too much for granted, and he did not intend to be blindsided a second time.

Mr. Admuson unscrewed the lid from the second jar of Null and Void and checked his watch. He nodded his head as if he couldn't agree more and pronounced it to be time for another dose of crow enhancement. Mew had worked up a good sweat but was still crooning. The crow lay there with his beak wide open, watching Mr. Admuson and the eyedropper and, if there wasn't a hopeful look of expectation in his little eyes, then I am no judge.

My dad was the first to remember poor old Mose outside all alone. He took the jar of Null and Void to the door and hollered. He didn't need to holler loud—nor twice. Mose accepted the comfort and promised my dad another star in his crown. After a long pull, Mose mentioned that it was mighty lonely and thirsty out there. Without making any outright promises, Mose hinted that if my dad felt the need for still more stars in his crown, a little more Null and Void, to carry out into that lonesomeness, might just do the trick.

While my dad was finding an empty coffee can and dividing the Null and Void with Mose, Ruby and Mr. Admuson had gotten their heads together and concluded that nobody could rightly expect a crow to heal in such a dreary place. So Ruby again brought out her old Harmony guitar and commenced singing a song I was too young to hear.

When my dad came back, he and Mr. Admuson took a lantern and went outside to pick a joyful bouquet of flowers for the sick room. That's when I learned another lesson: don't carry a lantern out on a dark night to pick flowers if Mose Washington is standing guard with a shotgun and a coffee can full of Null and Void. Almost before we heard the blast, Howard made sure he still had his butt and took off for his special secret hiding place among the tall sunflowers.

Mr. Admuson and my dad came indoors on the run—pale and sober. Sick crow or no sick crow, they said their good-byes and snuck out of that dark back door for their homes.

Mew had about crooned herself hoarse, and Mr. Strang was snoring with his head on his arms. He had started another page of his list, and the last word I could read was "Albatross."

The crow lay there with his beak open, quietly going "Caw, Caw," doubtless wishing good old Mr. Admuson would come back with his eye dropper. But nobody was paying attention. I stretched out on the butt-sprung sofa and hoped the day was over.

I was the second to wake next morning. Mew passed my bed, barefoot and quiet, carrying the crow, bright-eyed in her outstretched hands. When she opened the door, that old crow lifted itself right up into the air like it had never had anything more wrong with it than maybe a bad hangnail.

34

I can tell you it was pretty quiet around that house. Ruby was snoring gently in the rocking chair, and Mr. Strang was stretched out on the floor, still as a cast-iron bootjack. I figured that, after working most of the night at crow-healing, they would wake starved, so I determined to be a good Samaritan and prepare breakfast.

The first four eggs I broke into the skillet were destined for scrambulation. The next one showed some signs of sunny-side-upness but failed. The inside of Ruby's refrigerator made my mom's look like the failed hope of a starving family. Still and all, it appeared that Ruby did not have my mom's foresight. She had not laid in enough weenies to last the duration of the war. To my mom's way of thinking, since gasoline and sugar and rubber tires were rationed, it was just a matter of time before the government realized that the war might be lost if our boys overseas went unweenied. She said she wasn't hoarding; she was just being prepared.

It's blamed hard to fix a decent breakfast without weenies to fry, but meat was hard to come by, and even

Ruby was out of bacon and sausage. Still, there was a Sunday roast, so I figured I could make do. I scooted the eggs over to the side of the skillet because they were looking pretty well done, turned up the heat, and lay the roast in beside them.

Now, you might think that the smell of an elegant breakfast wafting through the house would have wakened those sleepyheads, but it didn't. Neither did the smoke that began to out-waft the breakfast smell. I say it in all modesty: anyone coming in blindfolded would have swore they were in my mom's own kitchen.

But Mr. Strang wasn't showing any signs of waking up. In point of fact, as the fellow says, he was showing very few signs of being alive. Aside from myself, the only interest being showed in life at all was being done by the eggs. They were browning up nicely. I added a couple more spoonfuls of lard and went home to clean myself up for running the route.

It was past normal when Mr. Strang pulled into our driveway, and he didn't look at all well. Out of the corner of my eye I watched for a portent that he had immensely enjoyed his breakfast, but he didn't seem to have a portent left in him. I didn't mind. Like the preacher says to do, I just kept my light hidden under a bushel and grinned to myself.

At least Mr. Strang didn't seem to remember what he'd heard last night. He didn't call me Walnut! He also didn't seem to remember that this was the day he planned to rid the world of a crow-sweated-unfit bed and buy a new one. No, sir, he mostly just drove the truck and moaned.

Even when I tried to cheer him up by singing "Pop Goes the Weasel," he moaned. I finally figured out that he was moaning on a pretty regular, steady, basis, which is called "tempo," so I worked my song to where

instead of a POP, Mr. Strang gave out a moan. I will tell
you this: if you ever set out to make a joyful noise unto
the Lord, don't omit the POPS. Likely as not the Lord
hears all the moans and groans he wants to.

It was a thing to ponder. I decided, right then and
there, that instead of ending my prayers with "Amen," I
would just say "POP!" If that didn't make Jesus happy,
maybe even make him grin a little, I would be very
much surprised.

Still and all, I was in the mood to sing. One old grump
in a panel truck makes it crowded enough. I just needed
to utilize what I had at hand, namely and to wit, moans
and groans. Now, see, stop and think about it. There
just aren't too many songs that include moaning and
groaning. 'Course, then I thought of slave songs, which
made me think of canebrake slaves—down there waiting and hoping for the advent of me and my steamboat
to come and set them free. That made me feel so guilty I
plain didn't feel like singing anymore. So I just shut up
and became grumpy. If I had had their address, I would
have just boxed up all the straightened nails and the
steam whistle and mailed them off with a note telling
those slaves to build their own damn steamboat.

But then I felt even more guilty, so I said, "Dear God,
please forgive me that unchristian thought. POP."

The "POP" was the only part said aloud, and I guess it
was pretty aloud. Mr. Strang jumped, and his elbow hit
the horn button. So he jumped again, and he said,
"Jesus Christ!"

"Yes, sir," I said. "Jesus Christ, POP."

Sometime during that long night, last night—during
the crow-healing, during the keening and the crooning,
the eye-rolling, the feathers—and the drinking of crow-
beneficent Null and Void, during the occasional
butt-be-gone shotgun blasts—Mr. Admuson and Ruby

had struck a deal. Ruby agreed to try distributing Mr. Admuson's product, Null and Void, along our route.

The route had been boring that day. I only broke one bottle of cream, and that was not my fault. The ancestors of the City Fathers had, plain and simple, built the curbs too high, too close to where a boy might reasonably be expected to be swinging a bottle of cream. I had seen their pictures, those Fathers of Fathers, there in the Masonic Hall, and if they gave a thought as to whether or not a fellow broke a pint of cream on their dingle-brained curbs, I would be very much surprised. Mr. Strang didn't say a word about the cream. He maybe groaned. I don't remember.

If you are a foreigner, someone not born and raised right here in the Little Balkans, then you likely do not know of the dangers involved in the vocation of making moonshine whiskey. The things that get you caught, the things that put you in prison for three years while your children endure the side-wise looks from Sunday School teachers. Well, let me tell you.

The smoke is mostly what gets you caught. The smoke and the smell, and the inordinate consumption of sugar.

Most moonshiners hide their stills and their caches deep in the timber, or in brush covered gullies, or in caves, or, especially in the Little Balkans, in mine shafts.

Mr. Admuson operated his still right at home in a hand-built cyclone cave. Understand now, Mr. Admuson wasn't stupid. He had his cave right in the middle of a large chicken pen. The chicken farm was his cover, just like the dairy with white-painted milk bottles was Ruby's cover. On the days when he worked his still he burned chicken feathers, and, I'll guarantee you, burning chicken feathers can overcome the smell of cooking corn mash any day of the week. Mostly it all worked pretty well, but there were some drawbacks. A lot of folks raised their own chickens and didn't need to buy them from Mr. Admuson. His great selling point was that when you bought one of his chickens it came at least semi-plucked. And if sales of Null and Void were particularly good, most of his chickens might just as well expect to face the world stark naked and see their plumage go up in smoke.

Mr. Strang made Admusons the last stop of the day and that was a good thing for me. My life was about to change. There on the back porch step sat Loris, cross-legged, barefoot, worrying a splinter in her toe.

Call me dumb and I won't argue. It's just that I had never thought about Loris, a certified albino, having toes. Catholic girls, yes. Arab girls, probably. And God alone knew about Chinese girls.

Mr. Strang had to nudge me to get me out of the truck, and then I just leaned on the fender and stared like a fool. All I could think of was that stained glass window in the Methodist church; the one where all the little children had been suffered to come unto Him. What I saw was Loris, sitting there worrying the luckiest splinter in the world. Around her wafted the incense of burning chicken feathers and cooking mash, and if that wasn't a pure and simple epiphany, then I just don't understand epiphanies.

My soul and breakfast, I might be in love.

I would have to think of a way to convince my dad to buy me a bottle of that red stuff the barber used to slick down my hair. I would likely have to learn to shave.

"All Mighty Heavenly Father," I whispered under my breath, "Him who delivered Daniel from the lion's den, the Hebrews from the fiery furnace, and other things too numerous to mention: thank you for Loris. POP."

35

I woke to the sound of my dad's singing: "Lord of harvest, grant that we, wholesome grain and pure may be." A Thanksgiving song, though it was still far and away from Thanksgiving. See, my dad tended to celebrate holidays at his own time and at his own pace. There was no way on God's green earth that I could know, on waking, if I should brace myself for Groundhog Day, Shrove Tuesday, or the Haymarket Riot. It never occurred to me to question. Like as not, someday I would have that responsibility.

Unlikely as it might seem, my mom usually went right along with this. She had more confidence in my dad's usurpatation of when a holiday might rear its ugly head than she had in the government's, or the Pope's.

So I smelled the sage and thyme and onion. I smelled the dressing, the stuffing which would be crammed into the fried weenies. My mom sang along, lagging a few beats behind because she could never remember the words exactly in their proper order. Truth to tell, my mom bluffed her way through the singing part of Thanksgiving.

Still, Thanksgivings are not as hard as Christmases. With Christmas songs you have to deal with Wise Men and livestock and frankincense, and get them all in the right place at the right time before the cock crows thrice. With Thanksgiving all you need to do is sing extra loud when it comes to the harvest being gathered in, and people will believe you know what you're talking about. You can forget about the Indians, although they brought the first begotten turkeys and the popcorn. Nothing rhymes with "Indian." But if you are determined to try to work in the Indians you should just mumble and let on that you have dropped the pot holder. So my mom sang along until my dad got to the part about where all and sundry were thankful for the "wheat and tares," and then she screamed, "Wilson, where in the world are the wheat and tares?"

It was the last straw.

At the last Thanksgiving, which had occurred about three weeks earlier, my mom had noticed and mentioned the paucity of tares. "Your son," she demanded, "is almost a man, and has never yet tasted a tare. I can not prepare a respectable Thanksgiving meal without a tare or two!"

My dad quoted Isaiah .015625: "And he who are without a tare may use a boiled egg."

I pulled on my yesterday's underpants, onto which my mom had embroidered "Wed," even though I would be wearing them on Saturday.

Like tares, clean underpants seemed to be a paucity, but, Isaiah or no Isaiah I could see no way to substitute a boiled egg.

Mr. Strang tapped on the new screen door with the pure and simple intent of picking me up to run the

route. He had no idea that he was about to encounter a
Thanksgiving. But see, anybody who habitually wears a
polkadotty bow tie, tenor-banjo-player striped pants
and peddles moonshine from white painted milk bottles
can deal with an abruptly declared Thanksgiving with
surprising ease.

See, Mr. Strang had learned the basic secret of life—
that is to say, the secret of social harmony—and I
learned it from him: "For that which we are about to
receive, we give thanks." That's all you need to know.
If a fellow says that, he is home free and clear. Matters
not a damn if it's celebrating the fastest train on the
Union Pacific Railroad or the third emperor of China's
bellybutton lint. Just say, "for that which we are about
to receive," and people will believe your heart's in the
right place.

So my mom wished him a joyous Thanksgiving and
inquired as to if he would like a boiled egg with his
stuffed weenie because, through no fault of her own,
there was a paucity of tares at the moment.

Mr. Strang admitted that since his brother-in-law,
Howard, had returned from Camp Leonard Wood and
started a Victory garden, he was about up to his eyebrows in paucitys—and tares—and zucchinis. He said
the seeds got under the plates of his false teeth and were
as aggravating as a stone granite rock. He said he would
drive clear to Wisconsin before he would go back to that
damn dentist in North Dinglebutt because you wouldn't
believe how bad seeds under a fellow's plates could be. If
that dentist in North Dinglebutt only knew! Mr. Strang
said he would be almighty grateful for a good old fried
weenie and boiled egg. He said you wouldn't believe how
stickery the seeds from paucities were, and blackberries
were even worse.

My dad brought out a pint of "Eau de la Fransay," a gift from Bert Henkinsiepen who claimed to have some French blood from his mother's side. Eau de la Fransay was made deep down in Mr. Henkinsiepen's lease of ground, which was a quarter of an acre at the top side but went down forty-six thousand miles which is why it had a sort of Chinese taste which added to the cost by one nickel per gallon.

By most anybody's standards our Saturday morning Thanksgiving breakfast would be declared a success. My mom's fried, stuffed weenies with a side dish of boiled eggs guaranteed her continued reputation as a cook. And my dad's thoughtful addition of the Eau de la Fransay guaranteed his reputation as a fellow who could be trusted to produce a holiday when one was required.

Mr. Strang delayed the route long enough to visit Steinberg's Emporium. With one front wheel of the Strang Dairy truck somewhat over the curb, the engine still running—growling, wanting more, maybe feeling cheated—we went in and Mr. Strang placed his order. For me he bought a polkadotty bow tie and a pair of flannel pajamas. For himself, he bought a double-note harmonica in the key of G.

36

Mr. Strang next aimed the truck in the general direction of the back door of the drugstore. We traveled just fast enough to keep the engine from dying, though it bucked badly in protest and made unchristian sounds. I didn't say anything, but I could feel its frustration. That engine had been designed to go from a dead stop to 65 miles an hour in eight minutes!

But Mr. Strang seemed to be in a mood of pleasant and thoughtful consideration. He was considering much more important things than the mechanical miracles wrought in Detroit, Michigan.

"Walnut," he said...

And I knew in a flash that I would not be thankful "for that which I was about to receive." He had called me Walnut! He had remembered! And, oh, my soul and breakfast, I had hoped he would not. Of all that he *might* have remembered from that night of crow healing—the feathers, the crooning, the lately lamented crow-sweat-soaked bed—all he remembered was that my dad had blurted out how my mom had christened me "Walnut."

"Walnut," he repeated, "On this joyous day of Thanksgiving, I stand before you, a thankful and humble man. I am thankful and humble because the Strang Dairy is the most admired and respected humble enterprise in all of Epic, Kansas! And I will whip any man who says otherwise.

"Still and all," he continued, "'Necessity is the mother of prevention,' as the fellow says, and we must maintain and improve our image. Henceforth, as we make our rounds, you shall wear your new Jazz-bow tie, and I will play my harmonica in the key of G."

"What about the pajamas?" I asked, knowing deep in my heart that, again, I was not going to be thankful for what I was about to receive.

"The pajamas!" Mr. Strang mulled and pondered. "Pajamas will be worn by all employees of the Strang Dairy because nobody on God's green earth wants to buy milk from people who sleep in their underpants." Before I could inquire as to whether or not people would buy milk from a fellow who slept without a polkadotty bow tie, the truck finally found, pretty much on its own recognizance, the back door of Emil Perkin's drugstore.

We delivered our Deep Shaft product at the back door in clear, gallon jugs. When it next saw the light of day, that Deep Shaft would be watered down and going out the front door in brown, half-pint, bottles labeled:

Dr. Perkins' Patented Remedy
For the guaranteed relief of Female Complaints
And toenail fungus.

Emil Perkins would be the first to admit that the men who bought the Remedy on a daily basis were less than enthusiastic concerning its curative powers in regard to complaining females. "Still and all," he would tell you, "toenail fungus is down eighty percent from three years ago."

Mr. Perkins bought an extra gallon that day, and Mr. Strang explained it was because Mr. Perkins had been impressed with the bow tie and the harmonica in the key of G.

"Pay attention," he admonished, "Learn all you can, while you can, because I will likely soon be called upon by an ivory league to teach in business college back East."

By the time we finished the route and got back to the dairy, Mr. Strang's Thanksgiving spirit had pretty much unraveled. It might have been the wearing off of the Eau de la Fransay, or it might have been the lingering memory of those little home-canned asparagues my mom served as a *piece-of-resistance,* but which looked too almighty like tomato worms to actually savor. The key of G harmonica lay in the crack between the seat and the backrest—its promise and potential forgotten.

Ruby had lured Howard out of his hiding place by threatening to blow his butt off did he not get busy repainting the white on the milk bottles. They stood, the milk bottles, drying in the sun. Howard, understandably distraught by his forced servitude, had gone down to the barn and was trying to teach the goats how to conjugate the verb "goddamn it."

Ruby brought in the last of the Moon Butter utensils for me to scrub and settled herself on the bench to admire my polkadotty bow tie. She said the tie set off my freckles and, taken all together, I plain outshined all the stars in the firmament. She said that when Loris saw me I would be a goner.

The watch-crow circled low, twice, misjudged the wind, skittered across a small patch of grass and landed, belly up, at Ruby's feet, pretending to be shot.

Those little toe-claws curling and uncurling in anticipation of a taste of Moon Butter or Null and Void.

"He's been that way all day," Ruby told me. "As if I don't have problems enough! I have a husband who can't tell his butt from Thanksgiving, and a brother who believes *his* butt is the focal point of the universe."

She laid the crow on the benevolence of her bosom and rubbed its beak with her nose. "Been crashing down all day, pretending to be shot! Remembering the pleasure of the healing, not the pain. All I need, a goddamn alcoholic crow!" She pulled an eyedropper from her pocket, and you would think nobody in the world was more surprised than she to find it there. You ever want to see a crow's eyes brighten, try a little Null and Void in an eyedropper!

See, that's the way Ruby is.

37

Sometimes, after supper, my dad and I sat by the cistern and straightened nails. We sat on the east side, where the sun wasn't too hot. Sometimes he tried to teach me words from his high school Latin: *per diem, per gratis.* We didn't talk anymore about building a steamboat, because that plan was far behind me, that was six weeks ago, when I was a kid. But we talked.

I was becoming rich working for the Strang Dairy. I knew I *looked* rich, because I wore a bow tie. My dad worried that I was beginning to look Republican. He didn't outright say so, but I could tell that he believed straightening bent nails was my only hope for salvation.

When we had straightened all the nails Mose Washington had given me, we drove around town looking for houses being torn down. Looking for bent nails. Now see, you might think we would be considered strange or eccentric—gathering bent nails in a syrup bucket, but my dad's reputation saved us. He had proved himself far and beyond being subjugated by screen doors. He also had a plan to move the Court

House a few feet to the south in order to make room for a steam whistle which would lighten the burden of mankind. And, let's face it, I wore a bow tie except when I was in bed. Precious few could find fault with us.

It never crossed my dad's mind to make me quit my job, even though he believed he might be nurturing a Republican at his bosom. No, sir, he just put an ad in *The Buffalo County Trans-Weekly Disciplinarian* offering to buy bent nails. "Any amount. Rusty or clean, just bent." I just guess most folks would be very surprised at how many people had been laying back their bent nails waiting for my dad to run an ad like that.

One day after stopping at Armageddon Mr. Strang continued south.

Dollar Denton had set up in Jericho, further south yet than Armageddon. Ruby had heard of him because he was gaining a reputation for making quality booze. Quality was the only thing Ruby would deal in. Mr. Strang had heard of him because Dollar Denton was gaining a reputation for cutting the price ten cents a gallon to make a sale, or cutting your throat for three cents to prove that he could and would.

Ruby cuddled the watch-crow and talked about how life in "The Business," in the Little Balkans, was rough and dangerous again—"like the old days," she said. "It's this goddamn war as did it," she said. "Sugar rationed—can't make alcohol without sugar. When booze gets scarce, it's worth more money, and more money means more fighting and killing. That's what brings out people like the Chicago Hot Shots and Dollar Denton."

You don't need to tell me that using the word "goddamn" is a sin. I know it is, and I only use that word when it is unavoidable. Still and all, anytime I heard Ruby preamble with *that word* I paid attention and learned. No doubt in my mind, if somewhere along the line one of my teachers had said "goddamn it, Wally, 6x6=36," I would have been saved a world of embarrassment later. So, little by little, without really meaning to, Ruby taught me the language and the trade.

Anyway, Mr. Strang and I drove down to Jericho to visit Dollar Denton. It wasn't that we needed more whiskey, it was that Ruby always liked to have what you might call a backup source. She sometimes bragged that no customer of hers ever suffered the "disappointment of disappointment."

Unlike Ruby and a lot of others, Dollar Denton, distilled his own product. He kept a rackety-shamble little grocery store there in Jericho as a front. Some of the cans on his shelves were swollen to the point of imminent explosion. Some of the paper sacks of flour and cornmeal had burst, and become a mousely equivalent of Mr. Roosevelt's Social Security. The bearded, kindly-looking man on the Quaker Oats box showed what could only be the beginnings of a goiter.

Mr. Strang said Dollar sold a sight more Deep Shaft than he did Campbell's pork and beans. A frugal man, Dollar Denton boasted to have the first dollar he ever made. You could see half of it, framed, behind his counter. The other half he had cut off and hidden where moths could not consume nor rust corrode.

As with all moonshiners, his still was hidden. Maybe it was far behind the dark side of the moon. Where? You didn't know and, unless you were a complete fool, you didn't want to know. If you are among those who believe a person can't become invisible, try inquiring, in the Little Balkans, where a fellow might find a still.

Mr. Denton didn't take to me at all. As subtle as I could I offered him the observance of my bow tie, but maybe he had seen bow ties before. Most of the people in the business did not want kids involved. Mr. Strang had to explain me—how I worked for Ruby and was a personal friend of Booger Red. It was only when I handed him a pint of Ruby's Moon Butter that Dollar Denton melted right down. "Wally," he said, "if I had a first-born son, I would give him to you *persona non grata!*" I smiled and appreciated his intent. But, truth to tell, if I brought home any first-born sons or any *non gratas,* my mom would crucify me dead and buried. She was already howling pretty loud about the growing pile of bent nails in the front yard. And once, when my dad asked, in a soft voice, would she rather have a pile of bent nails or a Republican for a son, she just said, "Jesus Christ," and went back to the kitchen. I'll say this for my mom, she could quote the Bible.

They struck some sort of deal, Mr. Strang and Dollar Denton. A time or two I tried to impart my knowledge as far as Japs and Nazis and the scarcity of sugar but, in all honesty, they likely could have gotten along without me.

Four days later Dollar Denton was dead; maybe not certifiably dead, but *gone.* If you are a Little Balkan moonshiner, and *gone,* then likely you are dead. *Gone* means that having a gold tooth didn't mean as much as you had hoped. *Gone* means you wasted your money buying that .38 caliber British Bulldog. *Gone* means no place to put a tombstone.

I asked Mr. Strang if Dollar Denton was dead. He felt for his collar button as if it had been there just a minute ago and now it wasn't, and why have a collar button you can't depend on? "Hell no," he told me. "He just bought himself a Lincoln Zephyr and drove to Chicago to buy himself a whorehouse."

I tried to think of him as not dead. At night I squeezed my eyes shut and tried to think of Loris, but all I could think of was Dollar Denton, floating face down right there along side of Sam Pullium in the cold water of a deep mine pit.

Mostly what I could remember was the deep pock marks on the back of his neck and the gold around some of his teeth. What I couldn't shake from my mind was the thought of those deep pock marks filled with cold mine-pit water. If you want to raise goose bumps on me, mention mine-pit water!

Nobody ever received a postal card from Dollar Denton saying, "Having a wonderful time; wish you were here." I'm glad I didn't. Still and all, it did me some good to remember I had given him some Moon Butter. I've never been pestered by ghosts, but with dead people, you never know.

38

It was good I had Loris to talk to. When I mentioned Dollar Denton to Ruby or Mr. Strang their mouths just pulled up into straight lines with little wrinkles up and down at the corners. Howard had stopped speaking to anyone except goats; and while I did speak some goat talk, Howard mostly ignored me.

My dad wasn't much help because he was busy philo-sophically juxtaposing bent nails and Republicanism.

Sweet Loris. She listened to how I hated dead people and offered, as recompense, to show me her splinter-punctured toe. I didn't say "Jesus Christ" in gratitude, because I was trying to break the habit. See, I was try-ing to balance it all out. I didn't want to go to hell for blasphemy, but it had been my experience that people with *too* much religion often had a dead mouse in their refrigerator when a fellow came to deliver the milk.

Still and all, of course, I couldn't tell Loris everything I knew about Mr. Dead Dollar Denton, because she was a girl. And it makes no sense, not even to me, but I didn't tell Purdy Grundy, my best friend, anything much at all, even though he was a boy.

Like as not I shouldn't have talked to Loris about the dying habits of moonshiners, because her own dad was one. But it's other people's fathers who die, not ours.

They say life goes on. I guess it does, at least somewhat.

When I got home, about suppertime, my dad was sitting, downcast, by the cool, brassy-smelling radiator of our Model T Ford. Dollar Denton wasn't on his mind. In point of fact, nothing was on his mind except that his own best friend of a car wouldn't run.

Ever since my dad and I dragged it from the chicken house and scraped off the reminders of chickens long gone, that car had run. My mom said that the way my dad loved that car "passethed all understanding." See, you had to know my dad and know that car to understand. Likely you have heard, "What God has joined together, let no man put us under." My mom didn't even bother to try.

I will tell you the truth, I couldn't get Dollar Denton out of my mind. It was likely unchristian of me, but I couldn't muster up much interest in a car that didn't run. I walked back over to the dairy. I'd just as soon be there as anywhere.

In the goat pen, just this side of the barn, Howard sat on a three-legged stool reading aloud his own translation of *The Billy Goats Gruff*. In all fairness, I'll have to give old Howard credit. His "baas" and his "bleats" were loud enough; and they seemed to come from the heart. Still and all, any goat in the world would tell you that Howard simply did not have much of a gift for the language.

I sat down on the step and listened to Ruby pull sounds out of her guitar that not one angel in a hundred could do. She asked me what was wrong. She could always tell, Ruby could, when something was wrong. I skipped over Dollar Denton and, instead, told her I figured my dad would likely perish before the dawn because of a terrible case of "Model T Despair."

Ruby laid her guitar down and shouted in the direction of the goat pen for Howard to shut up that noise or she would call Camp Leonard Wood and Leonard, himself, would come up and shoot his butt off.

Then she led me into the storm cave where she pushed some boxes around until she found what she wanted: a gallon jug. "It's double-distilled from pure Missouri sweet potatoes," she told me. Ruby tied a rope through the finger hole of the jug and fastened the other end of the rope onto a strong stick. She showed me how to carry it so it wouldn't come within three feet of my body. "Don't, whatever you do, let this break. It would eat a hole clear down to China, and, if there's one thing I don't need right now it's a bunch of Chinamen clamoring around complaining about their leaky roofs."

She told me to tell my dad to use some of that liquid to prime the cylinders on the Model T, and then pour the rest in the gas tank. She said, "Tell him to stand off to the side!"

As most people did, my dad followed Ruby's advice, especially the important part about standing off to the side; otherwise, I would have been half an orphan.

That old car started on the first crank. It popped and shivered, but it was ready to roll! My dad drove it up and down the road a few times to calm it down, and then we anchored it to the rose trellis with a chain. We laid railroad ties at the front and back wheels, and went inside. My dad sat at the kitchen table and explained that he would write a "Learned Paper" for the *Popular Science Magazine*. I watched over his shoulder as he composed the title: *The Advent of Alcoholism Amongst Model T Fords in the Little Balkans.*

Next morning my dad went over and negotiated a deal with Ruby for a supply of fuel for the car. In as much as it was showing a tendency to lift its rear wheels and spin its tires, and, in as much as the headlights refused to turn off and winked at every car it met, they agreed that the next batch should be watered down a mite. He broached, as the fellow says, the thought of greasing the wheel bearings with Moon Butter, but Ruby would have no part of it. She said that as much as she could use the sale, she could not in good conscience let such a thing loose on the highways of Buffalo County.

When my dad pulled away, that old car purred like a sixteen cylinder Cadillac. On the back floor boards sat a one gallon jug of Ruby's Superior. A double-distilled Deep Shaft with some of Ruby's secret magic added, Ruby's Superior was only for the strong of stomach and the heavy of purse.

39

With the car problem solved my dad was free to tackle his next challenge. He had not forgotten his plan to move the courthouse a few feet to make room for his proposed steam whistle.

"Just look around you," he said. "Everybody you see has sour looks on their faces! "It's pure and simple because of their frustration with life. Swollen tonsils! Inflamed knees! One good pull on the rope of a steam whistle and their woes would disappear."

He wasn't halfway to the highway when he turned around and came back for a second gallon of Ruby's Superior. "I'll need more," he explained. "The County Commissioners are all Republican. Give me a Commission of good Democrats, or even Socialists, or, for goodness sakes, Populists, and with one gallon of Ruby's Superior I could get the courthouse moved to Oklahoma City. With Republicans, I'd be lucky to convince them to nudge a spirea bush."

Don't think for a minute my dad hated Republicans. He couldn't hate anyone. He did joke about them a little though, maybe mentioning "cloven hooves." But then, in the next breath, he might say, "Judas Iscariot wasn't really a bad kid; he just fell into running with a rough crowd."

Ruby suggested Mr. Strang and I make the drive up to Less, to visit Reverend Claude Applehanz, who'd planned to spread the *per gratis* gift of Moon Butter on communion wafers. Without fear of contraception, I can tell you that Ruby had made a convert.

Like most preachers, I guess, Reverend Applehanz didn't mince words. He ground them and pulverized them until you could swallow them without a drink of water.

He explained that he had not yet exposed his flock to Ruby's Moon Butter because it was his bounden duty to shield his congregation from the iniquitous and perpendicular temptations of the Father of Evil. But, after using up a carton of communion wafers spread with Moon Butter himself, he felt it explicit to inquire as to its cost per bulk, or perhaps, per washtub. He inquired as to what other products we might offer, *per gratis,* to the enhancement of the work of the Lord.

Now see, the success of the Strang Dairy was not based solely on Ruby's demand for excellence of the product. It was also based on Mr. Strang's ability to out-bull-hockey anyone who came down the pike. If you were a hog raiser he would tell you about the time one of his hogs crawled through the fence and ate every strawberry between here and Woodson County. If you were a cattle man he would talk about the time three of his cows got the scours and ambled down Main Street at the Fourth of July parade causing complete discouragement to the marching band.

Still and all, it was when Mr. Strang reverted to Bible talk that he was at his best. To Reverend Claude

Applehanz he quoted from the book of *Additions and Corrections to the Minutes of the Last Meeting*: "And he who hath a camel or a vine and shareth the milk thereof, *per gratis*, shall be, in the eyes of the Lord, a crooked-footed, lame-of-shank stump-sucker, deserving *not* the Kingdom of Heaven nor little else."

Reverend Applehanz blinked twice and I blinked three times. Plainly defeated, the Reverend inquired as to the likelihood of putting a gallon of Blind Sorrow on the cuff. Mr. Strang told him, "Not on the cuff, not by your clerical collar, and not by the hair of your chinny chin chin!

Mr. Strang was, beyond doubt, ready to extol on the virtues of cash-on-the-barrel-head as confirmed by the writings of Saint Agnes the Almost Pure. But Reverend Applehanz anticipated and dug deeper into his pocket to find another quarter.

We turned south, toward Armageddon.

"Lame of shank?" I questioned.

He snaked the double-note harmonica from the crack of the seat and whacked the lint out against his knee.

He grinned. "Walnut," he said, "Beats the hell out of me."

40

I was sneezing because I was in love. Ruby said it was because of the goldenrod, but Ruby hadn't seen Loris in her parachute dress.

She stood there, Loris, bedecked in a silk dress made from a parachute. Her mother had made it. A gift from a far away uncle. She stood there, just west of the hollyhocks, an angel if I ever saw one. And I stood there, barefoot, in my overalls and bow tie, sneezing every time I took a breath.

There were buttons on that dress, front and back—and up both sides. God forgive me for even thinking about it but, on the off chance that Loris ever had to sneeze, then I don't know how she would do it without popping all those buttons. I don't really understand how girls work.

It was most likely illegal to have that many buttons on a dress when the Japs and Nazis were battling at our ramparts but, if you could have seen Loris in that parachute dress, you would have sneezed too.

I am also not quite sure what a rampart is, but I asked God to bless our soldiers and our boys at sea.

I knew I should say something about the dress. I had sense enough to know that a girl didn't just stand there, west of the hollyhocks, in a parachute dress on the off chance that someone might come along and sneeze. So I did what had to be done and said, "That-is-a-pretty-dress." Then, to take the edge off my presumption, I said, "You want to go look for turtles?"

She told me no, she did not want to look for any damn turtles, and I guess I will never understand women because she always seemed to enjoy looking for turtles before.

And then Purdy Grundy rode up and let his bicycle down on the gravel. And then he preformed an actual BOW! And then the rascal inquired as to if Loris had become a princess! I would have cleaned his plow right then and there, if Loris hadn't been there.

Now see, in all modesty I can tell you that when it comes to bowing I am no slouch. I don't claim to be a professional bower, not in any way, shape, nor form. Still and all, I had been in the school Shakespeare play last year and had been trained in the art. So instead of just flat out rendering Purdy Grundy's lard, I gave him such a bow as would make him look like what they call a "Poltroon."

And the words came to me.

"What light from yonder window breaks, you dumb ass, that thou cant'st tell a *Queen* from a ding-bing princess?" See, when provoked, I can talk Shakespeare as good as Mona Simmons and she is in the eighth grade.

Loris cast me a pleasant beam from her yonder-window-type eyes, and old Purdy Grundy just picked up his bicycle and rode away.

My soul and breakfast, given a bow tie and an education a fellow can do anything.

I walked back to the dairy with the taste of Shakespeare still in my mouth, and with some shades of the Bible. See, they are about the same. 'Thy vine withereth!' I should have told old Purdy. 'As unto thee as a sharp stick unto the lands of The Pharisees,' I should have told him. But I always think of these things too late.

Ruby was singing a song about how she was thinking tonight of her Blue Eyes who was sailing far over the sea. I just guess if she ever saw Loris in her parachute dress she would forget about Blue Eyes, but I didn't say so.

I got busy scrubbing the pots and pans. To tell you the truth, I didn't mind. Sometimes I ran my finger around a rim which Ruby hadn't quite scraped clean, and had a taste. The taste was a puzzlement. I always wanted more.

I went home feeling tired but good. My dad was sitting by the cistern straightening nails because he had shaken hands with a Republican and felt his soul endangered. I tried to tell him about Loris's parachute dress, and normally he would have talked about a parachute dress for three days. But he picked a fishing worm from the edge where the dirt goes up against the concrete and considered it. "In twelve million years, Wally, according to Darwin, this worm may be your grandfather."

41

Dead people bothered my dreams: Sam Pullium floating face down in pit water, Dollar Denton *gone*—which is maybe worse. Dead people and parachute dresses. Purdy Grundy was there in a sort of way—and an ugly wrinkled old fishing worm leaning on a cane saying, "Good morning, Walnut. How is my favorite grandson?"

Sometimes dreams are so bad you never want to sleep again. Sometimes they are so good you don't want to wake up. And sometimes you wake up trying to remember a taste or a smell. I mean no disrespect in any way, shape or form but, sometimes when I dreamed about Loris, I swear I could get a whiff of Eau de la Burnt Chicken Feathers, because of her dad's running his still and not wanting to get caught.

I woke knowing I was flat, pure-and-tee in love with Loris. I would have plighted my troth at the drop of a hat. But here I was, almost in the eighth grade. On a good day I could spell perpendicular and on a very good day I could locate the state of Brazil on the map, but I had never on God's green earth been advised as to how I might just go about plighting a ding-bing troth—even if I had one.

Anyway, if the smell I woke with was not a good deal more pleasant than the smell of a troth, I would be very much surprised.

The smell I woke with was the smell of a buttery crust filled with **Moon Butter**. It was just another dream.

On the way to Ruby's I was singing "Oh Beautiful for Suspicious Skies and Amber Ways of Grain." I was feeling proud, because it's not every day a fellow comes up with the greatest invention since Knute Rockne invented the football.

Moon Butter Pie! It was as real in my mind as a sore toe. Still and yet, when I explained it to Ruby she near laughed me off the front step. She thought it was the dumbest idea she'd ever heard.

We ran the route, Mr. Strang and I, and stayed longer in North Dinglebutt than normal because North Dinglebutt had been influxed by Presbyterians. Mr. Strang said if there was anything on earth worse for our business than an influctuation of Presbyterians, he couldn't think what it might be.

Mr. Strang blowed the truck horn until all those Presbyterians gathered around. It didn't take long.

My soul and breakfast, I just wish you could have heard Mr. Strang! There is not one angel in four-thousand and fifty-seven who can talk Presbyterian as good as Mr. Strang.

"Predestination!" he shouted. "It is written in the book of *Fluctuations* that what is made, is made because of God's *pre*ordained will! Deep Shaft whisky is as much a part of God's plan as is the gravel beneath your shoe and the little blades of grass that blow and blossom and wither beneath thy feet!"

Finally, with no lag in his talking, Mr. Strang balanced two little glasses on the front fender of the truck: one for the ladies and one for the gentlemen. He sent me to the grocery store for a box of crackers, which were supposed to represent the body of Christ, but they were out of crackers, so I bought a box of oatmeal and nobody seemed to notice the difference. Breaking his own rule concerning free booze, but looking down the road to the future of the business, Mr. Strang filled those glasses and refilled them. He poured Ruby's Superior, until you would have been hard put to find an unrepentant sinner within a mile and a half. A line was forming back in the direction of the depot. It was composed of them as were pretty sure they had been communioned but seemed to understand the importance of not taking a chance. Now see, it's this way. I give credit where credit is due. When Mr. Strang, not really a religious man, administered a sacrament, he matched the partakers sacrament per sacrament. I finally scrooched him over into the passenger seat and aimed the truck southward, toward Armageddon.

I let the clutch out a little too fast and Mr. Strang fell back. Then he half stood and pointed toward the sky. As we pulled away, he promised those Presbyterians that the lame would be halted and the halt would be lamed. He was willing to admit that dealing with the blind would take a little longer, but he was working on it.

Over his shoulder he hollered back that while he could not really speak for the Roosevelt administration, he was sure that if any lepers would step forward, they would be anointed.

Mr. Strang was absolutely pleased with himself. "Salvation, by the half-pint!" he told me, "This has got to be the best business in the world!"

I kept the truck mostly on the road in the direction of Armageddon. Mr. Strang lay back, considering the merits of *First Thessalonians* as opposed to *Second Thessalonians* and whether he should just sell the damn goats and be done with it and whether he should turn Howard over to the soldiers at Camp Leonard Wood and let them come up and blow his butt off.

Cedar Rump looked almost unpopulated. "As quiet as Judas's tomb," Mr. Strang said, still in a biblical frame of mind.

An Italian had been stabbed in I'llbedamned, and the Santa Fe railroad was building up the grade there where the highway crosses the tracks in Galenaville.

I finally got us to Armageddon, and there stood old Booger Red. I was happy to see him out of the hospital. He wore a big smile, and his face as red as the sun is when you have to get up in the morning and go to the toilet before you really want to.

Booger Red asked just what in the world was the matter with Mr. Strang because he had never seen him look so peaked. I told him that Mr. Strang had been having trouble with the Thessalonians. Booger Red told me that he'd had a little trouble with them also, and the next time he saw a Thessalonian in Armageddon he was going to kill the sucker.

In all modesty I will tell you that I got us back to the Strang dairy in pretty good shape. In all *honesty,* I will also tell you that the right front fender of a 1933 Ford panel truck is no match at all for a concrete W.P.A. bridge.

Ruby and I helped Mr. Strang onto the bed. It was the same bed he had foresworn because it had once been inhabited by a hairy brother-in-law and a sweat-bedampened crow.

She gentled me into a chair by the table where sat two slices of warm apple pie. One was for me and one for Howard. But Howard was not there because he had reconsidered the war and declared himself (*in absentia*) on the side of the Allies. But he would fight the war in his own way. He was out gathering limestone and pop bottles filled with goat pee to build a bomb. "Drop one of these suckers on them," he said, "and I just guess they will sit up and pay attention!"

42

Now see, you could stir Ralph Waldo Emerson and Tom Mix together for forty years and they would not be able to describe Ruby's first Moon Butter pie and do it justice. She had thought my idea over and decided to try it.

She gave me a tiny piece because she had no way of knowing what its effects might be. Ruby watched me closely as I took my first bite.

I knew, with that first bite, that if Heaven was anything even close to as good as Moon Butter pie then I would change my way of life to earn a place there. I would stop the bad habit I had gotten into of swearing and wash my ears without being told. Still and all, by my fourth bite, it sort of came to me that, as long as I could get Moon Butter pie, I might not need Heaven.

In most ways Ruby was completely different from any woman I had ever met, but in one way she was the same. She apologized for the food she had prepared. "The crust," she said. "is as hard as a rock in some places and mushy in others."

Well, see, I had heard *that* at every meal I had eaten since time insubmersible. So I remembered my father's words and said, "Ruby, if they had served pie like this at the Last Supper, Judas Iscariot would never have left the fold. No, sir, he would have just sat there, banging his fork on the plate and singing 'Blest Be the Pie That Binds.'"

Ruby blushed at that—the first and only time I ever witnessed. She told me I was a "silver-tongued young rascal," and that she would pray God to protect all girls from my abominations. Still and all, she cut me another piece of pie. She also cut a large piece for herself. I made a note in my mind to figure how to use an "abomination" for the best results, should the opportunity arise.

Ruby wasn't wrong about the pie crust though. It didn't come within a mile of the flaky-bakey things Mew Washington made. I figured that part of the trouble was Ruby's old stove. You didn't need to call in Sargent Preston of the Northwest Canadian Mounties to learn that the Pilgrims had banged it a few times too many on Plymouth Rock.

Don't get me wrong. I'm not criticizing the Pilgrims in any way, shape, nor form. I suspect if the King of England is roaring, right behind you, demanding you to come back home and become Episcopalian, you just don't pay too much attention if the kitchen stove gets banged against a rock. Plymouth or not.

Another thing different about Ruby was she listened when I talked. Most adults, when a kid offers a suggestion, are really thinking, "Just go away and stick beans up your nose." Then, when you do, they can say, "By the sweet bloody wounds of our Lord God, what made you decide to stick beans up your nose?"

But Ruby wasn't like that. She gave me full credit for the idea of Moon Butter pie. And she listened when I suggested she buy a new stove and hire Mew Washington to produce her Moon Butter pies.

Next morning Ruby wrapped what was left of the Moon Butter pie in a copy of *The Buffalo County Trans-Weekly Disciplinarian* and told Mr. Strang and me to deliver it to Mew and Mose Washington *per gratis.*

We ran the route, Mr. Strang and I. First, north to Less, where the Reverend Claude Applehanz was laid low by a dose of the shingles, which he claimed to have caught from a whore in Armageddon, and he said he would not go there again if you paid him.

In Cedar Rump, Ira Penchnoble was laid low because of a sprained ankle got from a game of Bocci ball played with some newly arrived Italians. He bought two gallons of Blind Sorrow and said he hoped to Christ he would never meet any Hungarians.

At Booger Red's place there was a fellow sitting at the bar, suffering from the plight of arthritis of the knee. He said it was God's reward because he had shot a German in the knee in World War One. He said it didn't seem fair because the fellow he shot was a foreigner. What the hell did God want?

Back at the dairy, Ruby and Mew Washington already had their heads together, plotting the domination of the earth, by means of Moon Butter pie.

43

The bomb Howard was building in the back yard made me proud to be an American. That Howard was a little strange could not be denied. Still and all, anyone who could conceive a bomb made of limestone and pop bottles filled with goat piss demanded admiration.

I will tell you this! Bomb builders as dedicated as Howard are few and far between. The bomb grew every day. Any fool could see that God was on our side or else why had He spread the fields with so much limestone? And the goats? I flat changed my opinion of them. You couldn't get within forty feet of the goat pen without smelling their enthusiasm for the American cause.

And I found comfort in the thought of that bomb. See, my dreams were not just bothered by dead bootleggers. Some nights I was in a field, scrunching my belly, hiding as deep into the ground as I could because the Japs and Nazis were marching over the hill with their bayonets shining. They were looking to kill me. But, with the bomb, my dreams changed. Howard was in the field with me, pointing his finger at that bomb, a mean look in his eye. See, neither the toughest Jap nor the toughest Nazi is going to go up against a pop bottle full of goat piss.

At the end of the driveway Ruby turned the truck south toward Armageddon. Mew sat in the passenger seat, and Mr. Strang and I sat on the floor behind.

The evening before, we had gathered around the kitchen table and sampled Ruby's second Moon Butter pie. There was myself, Ruby, Mr. Strang, Mew, and Howard. Outside, Mose stood guard with his shotgun. We were there to discuss the manufacture and sales of our new venture: Moon Butter pie. There was the question of a new stove. And that's why Howard was there—to present the case for keeping the old Plymouth Rock-dented stove. Howard maintained that getting rid of the old stove would be a victory for Episcopalians in general and the King of England in particular. Howard had never really liked the King of England.

The pleasure and responsibility of choosing the new stove was left up to Mew, and she chose a grand one. It was second hand from a restaurant gone broke. We found it in the show window of the hardware store and we almost had to beg to see it. See, it was draped over with canvas because it was so beautiful that people would just sit down on the sidewalk and stare at it. All nickel plated and green enameled—my soul and breakfast! It was a pure wonder. Mr. Strang suggested that the oven was big enough to roast a goat, but Ruby told him to shut his mouth.

Booger Red made the arrangements to have it hauled to the dairy and we went home to clear a space. Ruby gave the old stove to Howard and he was delighted. He started taking it apart immediately. It wasn't hard to tell how Howard's mind was working. If the King of England wants the stove, the King of England shall have the stove. Given the abundance of limestone and the proclivity of goats to do as they have always done, given the cast iron chunks of the Plymouth Rock dented-stove—after we whipped the Japs and Nazis, the King of England might be in for a nasty surprise.

The kitchen became Mew's own kingdom. She decorated it with bright feathers, and not even Ruby dared stick her head in while Mew was baking. Mew made her own improvements to Moon Butter pie, all for the better. The crusts Mew produced with that new stove would have made Saint Peter leave the Pearly Gate unguarded whilst he snuck down to Mew's kitchen and made promises he was not authorized to make.

Ruby didn't inquire. She was a great respecter of secrets. Ruby supplied the Moon Butter and other ingredients; Mew made the pies. Ruby cast around everywhere to buy sugar. She would buy it by the barrel or by the handful. But sugar had gone to war. Most people just don't realize how much sugar is required to fight Japs and Nazis. Mose was hired too, to stand guard with his shotgun because the Strang Dairy had become more than a dairy, it had become a gold mine waiting to be discovered.

Now, howsoever it came about, Mose and the watch-crow became friends. They were both paid in what my dad would have called the "Coin of the Realm." Had that "Coin" been dropped on the sidewalk it would not have made a chime sound. It would have made a splash sound. Mose tried his best to teach the crow "people talk" and I expect the crow tried its best to instruct Mose in the language of the crows. The best I can say is that when they *sang* together it was better than having a broken arm. Probably.

It was a noisy but happy time. In the kitchen Mew crooned over her pies. In the Moon Butter room, Ruby yodeled Jimmy Rodgers songs. Howard carried extra buckets of water to the goats in the hope of increasing their output in regards to war production.

All around the yard the watch-crow circled, sometimes flying and sometimes not quite. Still and all, he avoided colliding with most of the low branches and stumps. Mose was nearly blind but he fired his shotgun when it seemed the thing to do. I expect not one angel in a car load risked flying too close to the Strang Dairy.

44

Loris was accepted into Mew's kitchen without a thought or the blink of an eye. That's the way Mew and Loris had hit it off from the first. They understood each other, chattering away and laughing at secrets. You put an albino and a voodoo queen in a dark room and you can't tell the difference without striking a match.

We ran the route, Mr. Strang and I, and at each stop we offered a fork-full-bite of Moon Butter pie, *per gratis* as a sample. We went through three pies that way, and by the time we pulled back in to the drive at the dairy, Mr. Strang was arguing with himself if he should buy two more delivery trucks or three.

We had been home five minutes at the most, unloading things and cleaning things, when a big, black 1933 Auburn sedan pulled up behind us. "God O' Mighty!" Mr. Strang said.

As near as I can remember, that was the first time in my life I ever heard God's last name. I knew I would never tell my mother. If she knew that God was an Irishman she would never be able to show her face in town again.

That was also the first time I really understood how Howard felt when he thought about those soldiers coming up from Camp Leonard Wood to blow his butt off. I had been cussing like a trooper and ignoring the Beatitudes in a shameful manner, and I didn't have any excuses ready for God. But it wasn't God who climbed out of the back seat of that car, it was Welsh Mary, a bootlegger from Nineveh. She was pretty in a mean sort of way. She had teeth which looked dangerous, which commanded caution. No doubt in my mind, had her foot been caught in a trap, she would have chewed her leg off at the ankle and gone about her business. Still and all, she managed a smile. "Nice bow tie," she told me.

Nineveh was a town of about two dozen families who earned their daily bread by mining lead and killing each other. Welsh Mary provided the liquid encouragement needed for both endeavors. I had never seen her before because Nineveh was Welsh Mary's territory like Epic was Ruby's territory.

All I knew about Welsh Mary was what I had heard from my dad. He said she had smashed her husband's head with a crowbar and walked away free when the Coroner declared it was the worst case of appendicitis he had ever seen. Nobody messed with Welsh Mary.

Now, if you can picture a landlord going up to a door with an eviction notice in one hand and a bouquet of roses in the other, then you can see Welsh Mary that day. Maybe not used to being sweet, maybe determined to try it once.

But I will tell you this: smashing a head or two and running a big bootleg operation does not necessarily prepare a person to be greeted at the front door by a mile-high black voodoo queen and a snow white glassy-eyed albino.

Still and all, that's what happened.

They took each other's measure, as the fellow says, Mew and Welsh Mary. Loris stood behind Mew giving that scary, hollow stare that made her look like a blind girl. I wanted to touch that Auburn car, but the gold-toothed driver gave me a growl from so deep down that it likely cracked some of his ribs. I ran to the Moon Butter room to get Ruby.

Dressed in her finest, nobody would have mistaken Ruby for a star of stage, screen and radio. In her work clothes, waddling out of the Moon Butter room? Well, the stoutest heart would have blinked twice.

Ruby paid no mind to her appearance. She offered her hand to Welsh Mary and Welsh Mary took it like they hadn't seen one another since the eighth grade. Likely because I was the only one on the horizon wearing a bow tie (Mr. Strang had wandered in the direction of the barn carrying his double-note harmonica in the key of G) and because I was not a voodoo queen nor an albino, Ruby suggested I cut a couple of slices of Moon Butter pie and "pour a little" for the entertainment of our guest.

Ruby guided Welsh Mary, by the elbow, around the corner of the house into the shade. Guided her away from the heat of the kitchen, voodoo queens, and albinos. Guided her into the shade where the only available view was that of a broom-skinny fellow with a black beard building a bomb out of limestone rocks and goat piss.

I stayed in the close-nearby, priding myself not so much on wanting to eavesdrop as on being available should my services be required to relinquish common courtesy. I suppose having viewed Ruby in her natural state, the sight of a limestone-goat-piss bomb builder was not an experience which would take any more years off Welsh Mary's life. And so, Welsh Mary accepted the pie along with a small—what they call in the French talk—"damn-its-ass" cup of Ruby's Superior.

Now, serving in those little damn-its-ass cups bothered me some. Ruby might not approve because those little cups had belonged to her grandma in the deep south.

And that reminded me that I had been woeful in not building a steamboat to free canebrake slaves.

The sun was nearly down when they struck a deal, Ruby and Welsh Mary, for the distribution of Moon Butter Pie in the Little Balkans. There could have been a feud, what they call a turf war. But Ruby held most of the best cards, and Welsh Mary knew it.

Welsh Mary held the control of her what they call "Dominion." They sat with their heads close together, sometimes shaking them up and down and sometimes sidewise.

In the end it would prove to be a gold mine, and, unbeknownst to me, I went home that evening about to become the richest boy in Buffalo County. Ruby had goddamned-it so many times that Welsh Mary finally gave in. I was declared a partner with all the rights, privileges, whereto-as's and hitherto-fore's as applied and implied by the law and all which pertains—with liberty and justice for all, and what God hath joined together let no man put us under.

See, that's the way Ruby is.

45

By the time I got home the County Commissioners had all left. There was little evidence that the most important meeting ever held in Buffalo County had been held there, right beside our own rose trellis.

Those in attendance were, as *The Buffalo County Trans-Weekly Disciplinarian* liked to say, "our most noble and selfless citizens."

The Commissioners were, as my dad liked to say, "the dumbest bunch of mule-headed Republicans this side of Istanbul." Still and all, my dad had woefully underestimated the amount of Ruby's Superior needed to move the court house—even a few feet.

Whether it was the Ruby's Superior or the County Commissioners which attracted the mosquitoes, I likely will never know. Maybe it was a combination of the two.

Maybe it was a combination of the *three* which attracted the purple martins.

My dad told me later that it was a tribute to the purple martins that they dive bombed the Superior, the County

Commissioners and the mosquitoes without prejudice.

What with the running out of Ruby's Superior, what with the mosquitoes and the dive bombing purple martins, the County Commissioners voted to move the Court House only seven inches to the south, and got the hell out. This was a disappointing compromise for my dad, who had figured it should be moved at *least* two feet.

I found my dad at the kitchen table with a pencil and two pieces of paper. He was creating—inventing again. The first plan was for a new bird: much like the mosquito-eating martin, but, still and yet, my dad's new bird was being designed to eat County Commissioners in the specific, and Republicans in general.

On the second piece of paper, he was sketching out a bronze plaque acknowledging himself as the one who had contributed untold gallons of Ruby's Superior for the benefit of the citizens of Buffalo County. (Date to be filled in later.)

Epilogue

Purdy Grundy caught the Infantile Paralysis, and I wished to God I had never whipped him where my dad obliterated the screen door.

In the doctor's investigation of what might cause Infantile Paralysis, he discovered that good old Purdy had spent a part of his summer straightening nails. In due course, as the fellow says, I was interviewed. I tried to explain about the canebrake slaves and the need for a steamboat and the need for straight nails, but I was ignored.

The Buffalo County Trans-Weekly Disciplinarian ran, in big letters, "Mothers, don't let your children straighten nails!"

Judas Priest.

Purdy got well—for the most part. But his left foot did not really keep up with his right foot.

Mr. Strang had his stroke on the same day the war ended. I was out whooping it up, listening to the church bells ring and the siren from Epic's fire truck.

He died, Mr. Strang, three days later, and I was glad. Oh, I cried, but I was glad. How the hell does a thing like that work? Crying and glad? Still and all, it didn't seem right for a tenor-banjo-pants-wearing man to lie stricken and crippled.

He was buried with his double-note harmonica lying on his chest, an almost-smile on his face.

Even though it was the Atom Bomb that won the war, Howard was granted a presidential pardon for his work in national defense. Although, to the best of my knowledge, the terrible Limestone-Goat Piss bomb has never been used.

With the war ended, pool tables were no longer on the list of rationed items. Booger Red splurged and bought two of them. He was always open on Sunday mornings and some say that's why the Methodist church in East Armageddon shut down.

Sister of Equanimity soon took over the management of the pool tables and enforced such an honest game that it was no longer fun. And so the Methodist Church opened up again until the termites came and chewed off the south end of the building.

Ruby bought the first new panel truck available in Buffalo County. It was red with clean white letters printed on it saying STRANG and WALLY DAIRY. She looked at me and said, "Wally, you could easy pass for sixteen—or at least fifteen—or, maybe fourteen."

She brought out her Kodak and took a picture. Loris is off there to the side, grinning, a little out of focus—still and all, if you know her, you'll recognize her.

That's me, behind the steering wheel, grinning. The front wheels of the new truck are turned to the left, headed south. Headed south toward Armageddon.

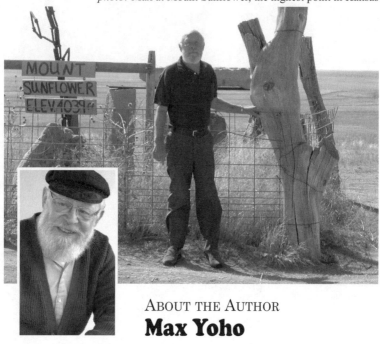

photo: Max at Mount Sunflower, the highest point in Kansas

ABOUT THE AUTHOR
Max Yoho

Born in 1934 in Colony, Kansas, Max grew up in small towns. Moving with his family to Atchison at age 10, he soon learned that delights and adventures along the Missouri River awaited just outside the well-oiled hinges of his bedroom window screen.

Max graduated from Topeka High School and attended Washburn University in Topeka, where he was a feature writer for *The Washburn Review*.

A former milk delivery boy himself, after a thirty-eight year career as a machinist Max retired in 1992 to begin a new career as a writer. His first novel, ***The Revival***, won the J. Donald Coffin Memorial Award of the Kansas Authors Club in 2002. ***Felicia, These Fish Are Delicious***, his collection of poems, essays and short stories, was nominated for this same award in 2005.

Books by Max Yoho

- *The Revival*, 2001
- *Tales from Comanche County: The Peculiar Education of Max Freeman*, 2002
- *Felicia, These Fish Are Delicious*, 2004
- *The Moon Butter Route*, 2006